GALACTIC JUNK DRAWER

SPACE JANITOR SHORTS

JULIA HUNI

IPH MEDIA

ORBITAL OPERATIONS

ONE

WITH THE HUGE crowd packed into the Level 82 concourse, Agent Tiberius O'Neill feared the station would explode. Or run out of air. He knew it was ridiculous, but the idea of this many people crammed into a paper-thin tin can in the sky almost made him hyperventilate.

"Looking a little pale, Griz." Agent "Vanti" Fioravanti glanced around the room. She looked casual, but O'Neill knew she was evaluating and cataloging every person and exit on the level. Vanti could spot a troublemaker a kilometer away, and her ability to analyze a situation had been legendary in their academy class.

"I'm OK," O'Neill lied. "I just haven't gotten my space legs, yet."

Vanti's lips twitched. "That's right, you've never spent much time in orbit, have you?"

"That's why I didn't volunteer for station duty." But they'd tapped him anyway. O'Neill had grown up dirtside, and his first experience in space had been the flight to Sally Ride to go to the academy. He hadn't enjoyed it.

Station Kelly-Kornienko orbited the planet Kaku. The eighty-three Level behemoth provided retail, manufacturing, recreational, and living space for thousands of people. It was also the home of most of the SK'Corp board of directors—wealthy oligarchs who controlled much of the settled galaxy.

"Look alive people." Commander Entebee's voice spoke quietly in

3

O'Neill's aural implant. "The board will be entering shortly. Take your stations."

O'Neill glanced at Vanti, giving her dress uniform a once-over. Every crease, button and medal sat exactly where it belonged, of course. A stray thread wouldn't dare cling to Vanti's uniform. He felt silly in the gold trimmed formal and hoped he looked half as professional as Vanti. She brushed a bit of lint off his collar, and they marched to their designated positions in front of the low stage erected at the edge of the circular concourse. A set of stanchions hung with velvet ropes marked off a corridor from the stage to an ornate golden door set in the wall between the float tubes. Red carpet stretched from the door to the stage. Two more agents stood at the far end, near the door. At O'Neill and Vanti's appearance, the crowd quieted expectantly, all looking toward that closed door.

"Not that we're worried about the crowds today, right?" Vanti said. O'Neill glanced across the stage at her, but Vanti's eyes never left the crowd. "A hand-picked audience rarely causes trouble."

"Are you saying we're just here for appearances?" O'Neill wasn't as good at sub-vocal communication as Vanti, but he was learning. Speaking without moving your jaw or making any measurable sound took practice. Vanti, of course, was an expert.

A tiny snort came through his implant. "They picked the two best looking agents in the office, even though we have almost zero real-world experience. What do you think?"

"I think you've got an ego like a gas giant." Although she was right about their lack of experience. They'd both ranked in the top ten of their academy class, but this was their first real assignment. So far, patrols of the station had been completely routine and boring. As far as appearance—with her smooth red hair, sparkling green eyes, and pale skin with just a sprinkle of freckles—Vanti was one of the most attractive agents in their unit. Although he wouldn't claim to be the best-looking guy in the service, he knew his dark, curly hair and chocolate brown eyes appealed to some people. And they were both young—actually young, not artificially young. He had to admit, Vanti had a point.

The crowd seemed docile, too. Based on appearances, most of them occupied the upper, more affluent levels of the station. With the exception of a few cargo handlers in suspiciously clean uniforms, and a small group of clearly uncomfortable station employees huddled near the back, everyone was well-groomed and expensively clad.

The ornate door slid open, and the crowd began to applaud, as if on cue. A dozen impeccably dressed men and women strode through. As they approached, O'Neill silently ticked them off in his mind, matching them to the pictures he'd memorized when he arrived on station.

Don Ahmed Ryan Smith led the way, nodding regally as he strode between the velvet ropes. His hooded eyes surveyed the crowd coldly. As chair of the board of directors, Smith was the most influential person on the station, and he clearly relished that position.

Behind Smith came the rest of the directors: Dame Zuckerberg, Don Putin, Dame Morgan and her teen daughter, Annabelle, Don Bezos and his drunken son Nicolai, Dame Buffet, Don Said, and Don Gates. The last in line, ancient Don Huatang, rode in a float chair, accompanied by his voluptuous and bored-looking granddaughter, Gloria. The group made their way onto the stage, and the applause died as quickly as it began.

O'Neill suppressed a shiver. These people were his employers, but they gave him the creeps. Thanks to aggressive and expensive esthetic treatments, none of them—even those with teenage children—looked a day over twenty-five, except Don Huatang, whose treatments appeared to have all given out at once. He looked to be about two hundred.

Smith stepped forward, the cam drones focusing in on his perfect, smooth face. "My dear friends, thank you for coming." His sonorous, probably specially engineered, voice rolled over the crowd, warm and welcoming. "The board and I have an exciting announcement to make. This has been a banner year for the company and the station. Profits are up. Production is up. People are happy."

The crowd cheered. "They're getting prompts from their holo-rings," Vanti muttered.

"Really?" O'Neill glanced at her, then out at the crowd. He let the voice drone on, listening only to tone, and watching the people. A moment later, Smith's voice paused, and a brief message flashed on every holo-ring. A cheer erupted from the crowd. O'Neill glanced at his ring and shook his head. Apparently, security agents were meant to be décor, not the cheering section.

"And so, today I am proud to announce that all station employees are now owners! Special stocks have been issued to each of you to confirm your ownership in our great company. Check your holo-rings!"

Around the room, holo-rings flashed. People turned to their neighbors, whispering and questioning. Cheering broke out in earnest this time, with some people laughing or even shedding tears.

"It's a LIE!!" A voice rose above the babble, amplified in some way. People stopped talking and turned toward the shout.

"They say they're giving you stock!" A tall, thin man in wrinkled clothing shoved through the crowd, pointing an accusing finger at Don Smith. "They claim they're giving you ownership in the station! They haven't told you what it will cost you! Look at your pay rate! For everyone one of you, it's going down! They're not giving you ownership; they're cutting your wages!"

The two guards at the float tubes stared at the man, frozen. O'Neill glanced around, but no one seemed to know what to do. The cheering stopped, and the whispering grew louder. "Commander Entebee?" O'Neill tried the comm, but it was down. He glanced at Vanti. She looked back, baffled.

The man pushed through the front row people, knocking one of the stanchions over. He stomped over the rope, yelling. "This 'special stock' is a farce! The total value is only one tenth of one percent, shared among ALL OF YOU!"

O'Neill glanced around again then stepped forward. "I'm going to have to ask you to turn off the amplification."

The man rounded on O'Neill. "You stooge! Don't you know they're using you?" He tried to push past, but O'Neill stepped in front of him. "They're using all of you!!" O'Neill yanked his holo-fryer out of his belt pouch and slapped it onto the man's hand, pressing the button.

"You—hey, what happened to my amplification?" The man yelled.

"I'm sorry, ser, but you can't just barge in here and start a riot," O'Neill said. "Now, if you'll come with me, I'll make sure your concerns are passed on through the appropriate—aagh." The edge of the man's hand slammed into O'Neill's throat.

The man shoved O'Neill away and lunged toward the stage. With a flash of copper hair, Vanti whirled across the room. Almost in slow motion, she flew off the ground, spun around and kicked the man in the head. Her other leg slammed into his gut, and he dropped to the ground. Vanti landed lightly beside him and had a cuff on his wrist before O'Neill could find his taser.

Up on the stage, Smith stared down at them. For a second, he appeared uncertain; then he amped up the charm. "Let's hear it for our brave security agents!"

The crowd cheered obediently. Smith launched back into his prepared speech. O'Neill gestured to the guards at the gold door, and one of them trotted down the red carpet. "Erzwith, I can't get the commander on the comms, can you?"

Agent Erzwith's eyes widened. "No, I can't. That never happens!"

"Calm down," O'Neill whispered. "Take this rabble-rouser down to holding in Level 1. On the way down, stop at the command center and have them send up more people. Take Maguire too. Make sure this guy doesn't get away. They'll want to question him."

O'Neill turned to Vanti. "You stay here, and I'll stand guard by the door. We'll get the board out of here as quickly as possible. Then we'll meet down in the commander's office."

Maguire and Erzwith hauled the man up by his arms and dragged him off to the float tubes. Vanti and O'Neill took up their new positions, but by that time, Smith had finished his speech. The board paraded back to the gold door, smiling and waving, except Dame Morgan's daughter, who narrowed her eyes and glared at Smith's back as she followed. Gloria Huatang gave O'Neill a suggestive once-over and a wink as she walked by.

Smith stopped by the gold door, a hand going to his throat. He stumbled and fell against the wall, his other hand clutching at his chest. Someone shrieked. Smith's face turned blue, and he collapsed on the red carpet.

Dame Morgan sank to her knees and put a hand on his chest. "Gates, call medical." She looked around the room and focused on O'Neill and Vanti. "He's not breathing. Are you trained in emergency medical treatment?"

"We can do basic evaluation and emergency resuscitation." Vanti dropped down next to Morgan, her hand going to Smith's neck to check the pulse.

"Medical will be here in sixty seconds," Don Gates called out.

» «

COMMANDER ENTEBEE PACED AROUND the conference room, fiddling with his shirt cuff. "They don't know what killed him," he said. "It can't have been the protester. Why would he make all that fuss if he was able to kill Smith that easily?"

"LeGrande," Vanti said. The commander gave her a questioning look. "That is the protester's name: LeGrande."

"It could have been a distraction." O'Neill rubbed his hand over his face. They'd had this exact discussion half a dozen times, including the commander forgetting the prisoner's name. "Maybe a partner did something while we were all focused on LeGrande."

Vanti sighed, shaking her head. "Nothing on the vid feeds, and they were pointed at Smith the whole time. Look, ser, we're not getting anywhere. Can we just take a break and come back to this later? Let me and Agent O'Neill go back up to the crime scene and see if we can find any additional clues."

"I hate investigations," Entebee muttered. "Life is so much simpler when you just have to stand guard and glare at people."

O'Neill and Vanti exchanged glances. This was their first real interaction with the commander, and he appeared to be an idiot. They'd been trained in investigative techniques at the academy. Most of their teachers enjoyed this kind of challenge. They'd expected a high-ranking officer would also. "Is there someone we can call in to help?" O'Neill suggested.

"And let them think I can't do my job?" Entebee's face turned bright red. "You two better figure this out, or you'll be headed dirtside in irons before you know what hit you!" Entebee's holo-ring buzzed, and he flicked the comm open. "What?"

"Ser, we think we know what killed him." A middle-aged woman with bright eyes and a saggy chin—sure sign of a cheap regeneration job—peered excitedly from the holo. "Nanobots!"

"What?" Entebee flopped down in a chair. "You mean like the things they use to color people's hair and skin? How could nanobots kill him? That's like saying he was killed by a makeup brush!" Entebee definitely wasn't the hottest star in the galaxy.

"He was injected with nanobots that could be triggered to stop his heart. We managed to isolate some. The programmers say they could have been in his system for hours or even days before being triggered. They were designed to do the job when triggered, then dissolve. But whoever designed this attack didn't realize the bots would stop reacting properly once the host was dead. So they didn't dissolve on schedule."

"Is there any way to track these nanobots back to their source?" O'Neill asked. "Any kind of marker?"

Entebee nodded enthusiastically. "Yes, good idea, O'Brien."

"O'Neill," Vanti snapped. "Ser, why don't you let us handle this? I'm sure there are other things only you can attend to." She smiled, giving him a fawning smile that didn't reach her eyes.

"Right." Entebee heaved himself out of the chair, frowning at the woman on the holo. "Collins, work with O'Brien and Fieroganti on this. I need to talk to Dame Morgan." He flicked the vid over to the room connection and stomped out the door.

"Sure, he remembers her name," Vanti groused under her breath.

"Who? Dame Morgan? She's a board member. He knows who signs the paychecks," Ty muttered back.

The woman in the vid smiled tiredly at them. "I'm Dr. Isabelle Corwin."

"Ty O'Neill." He pointed at himself. "And she's 'Vanti' Fioravanti."

"I need to run some more tests, and I'll get back to you on tracking these." The woman reached forward to flick off her holo-feed but stopped. Glancing around the room, she made a little face and leaned in close to the cam. "In case you were wondering about the commander's 'qualifications,' uh, well, he's Don Gates' cousin."

TWO

"I CAN'T BELIEVE you let them talk me into this!" Vanti paced around the tiny compartment, shoving her hands through her hair. The wavy strands, bleached a dirty blonde color, fell around her face. "I joined the academy to get away from this lower-lev lifestyle." She glared at the dingy walls, the worn sofa, then threadbare carpet.

"Hey, I didn't 'let' them do anything! You agreed on your own. It's not like we really had a choice, anyway." O'Neill snapped the metal latch hook into the loop set into the wall. He climbed down from the rickety futon, afraid it would collapse if he stepped in the middle. At the other end, he stepped back up, snapping the other hook into another loop on the opposite wall. The hammock swung gently above the futon, casting wavering shadows below. "I'm not entirely sure how I'm going to get into that thing, but it's up."

Vanti glanced at the hammock but didn't stop pacing. "Fan-fraking-tastic work, Agent O'Neill. Or should I say Mikael Leland? I think I'll call you Mick. That sounds like something a 'Lisa' would call her partner."

"Vanti—"

"Lisa," she snapped.

"Lisa, calm down. We're undercover. You would have begged for a chance to do this when we were at the academy."

"Going undercover is supposed to be glamorous, not tatty." Vanti looked at the futon again, then moved over to the counter and leaned against it instead.

"Welcome to the real world." O'Neill flopped down on the futon, raising a puff of dust. "You can sleep in the hammock if you want. I think it's cleaner."

"Ugh. I'd rather sleep on the dusty futon. Hammocks make me motion sick." She dropped down next to O'Neill, coughing dramatically. "Do you really think we'll be able to discover anything they don't already know?"

O'Neill shrugged. "Don Said seemed to think so. Dr. Corwin said the nanobots were created on station. The informant pointed them to this esthetician. And while we're investigating, we can also gauge the general climate here in the lower levels. If there are more people who feel like that protester, the board needs to know."

Vanti looked around the room, as if searching for someone eavesdropping. "Do you think he was right? I mean, from what I've seen of Smith, promising worthless 'stock shares' to offset pay cuts sounds like something he'd do."

O'Neill shifted uncomfortably. His whole life, he'd been taught to support the chain of command. His gut reaction was to believe in those in charge. But in the few weeks they'd been on station, he'd heard too many rumors about Smith. And then there was Entebee. That guy should have been standing guard at a munitions bunker, not commanding a station unit. His faith in the chain was starting to wear thin. "Our mission is to track down those nanobots, not to investigate the board."

"Right. The mission." Vanti jumped up again and crossed the five steps to the far side of the compartment. "Why don't you practice getting into that hammock while I stand way over here?"

It only took five tries to get into the hammock. On the fifth try, he got in, but flipped right back out. He landed flat on his back in a puff of dust, the wind knocked out of him.

"Are you sure you don't want the hammock?" He gasped for breath on the futon.

Vanti leaned against the counter, gasping for breath from laughing too hard. "Nope, you got this. You were almost there."

The sixth time was the charm.

» «

THE NEXT MORNING, O'Neill discovered getting out of the hammock was nearly as difficult as getting in. "This explains why the futon is in such terrible shape," Vanti said, after he finally resorted to swinging until he flipped out onto the dusty padding.

"I'm spending my first paycheck on a bunk bed," O'Neill grumbled, shuffling into the tiny bathroom.

When he came back out, Vanti handed him a protein bar. "I made breakfast."

"We have an AutoKich'n. It must make eggs and toast. Or cereal."

"I don't know. I don't eat that stuff," Vanti said. "Besides, you're running late for work, Mick."

"You don't eat eggs and toast? I would never have signed a domestic contract with a woman who doesn't eat toast." O'Neill opened the door and led the way down the hall toward the radial corridor.

"No, I don't eat bad AutoKich'n food." Vanti grimaced. "We only had the most basic food maps when I was a kid, and I vowed I would never go back after I got a decent job. That's what kept me in school, even when I hated it."

O'Neill glanced back at her as they stepped out onto the concourse. Vanti never talked about her family or life before the academy. And she seemed to love even the worst parts of academy life. "So, what do you eat, then?"

"Mostly takeout. And salads. You can get some good deals at the farmers' market on Level 25. And I've purchased a couple really expensive maps for special treats. Strawberry gelato from Saerdi's. Eggs benedict by Chef Mingtu Verazian." Vanti sighed and took a bite of her protein bar. "I'd rather eat these than cheap AutoKich'n eggs."

"Lots more food choices on the surface," O'Neill said, stepping into the float tube line. At shift change, the float tubes clogged up a bit. He made a mental note to leave the compartment earlier tomorrow.

"Yeah, but dirtside agents don't get paid as well," she replied. "I'll suck it up a few years and save up some credits."

They took the float tube up to Level 9. "I'm going to chat up the other business owners here while you get to work, sweetie." Vanti kissed him on the cheek.

"Sweetie?"

"It's our cover," she whispered. "We're supposed to be contracted. That means pet names and kissing."

O'Neill eyed her. He usually thought of Vanti as a work partner, not a woman. But she was pretty, and fit, and—smack! Vanti slapped him on the back of the head.

"It's our cover. Don't let it go to your head." She blew him a kiss and walked away.

"I should have made her get the job," O'Neill muttered as he knocked on the plasglas door of Doable Do.

A stick thin man in a black skin suit waved the door open. A shock of lime green hair grew in a fringe above his forehead and curled out over his eyes. The rest of his head and face shone like polished brass in the glare of the overhead lights. Drawn on eyebrows hovered over piercing orange eyes. Matching orange lipstick highlighted his perfect bow-shaped lips.

"Are you Mikael Leland?"

O'Neill smiled and held out a fist to bump. "Yeah, call me Mick. How are you today?"

The man shook his head. "This just won't do. Turn around."

"What?" O'Neill dropped his hand to his side.

"Turn around." The man made a spinning motion with his hand. "I want to see what I have to work with."

O'Neill turned slowly in place. "Why am I doing this?"

"Consider it part of the interview." The other man looked him carefully up and down as he spun. "I'm Taban. Moirrey told me you'd be coming by. I get final approval on all stylists and assistants in my shop. And right now, I'm thinking..." he paused for a long moment, "no."

What? No one had mentioned an interview. The job was supposed to have been a done deal, set up by one of the unit's contacts. "Uh, I thought I would be working for Moirrey?"

Taban heaved a dramatic sigh. "You would be. But I get final approval on all new employees. You must meet the esthetic standards of my salon to be hired."

O'Neill looked at him. The man ran a mediocre salon on Level 5, and he claimed to have standards? He raked his hand through his darkened hair. "Do I need a haircut? What are the standards?"

Taban ran a loving hand over his own knobby ribs and convex stomach. "I suppose your face is adequate. But, you need to have the body. I can't see anything with that," his face wrinkled in distaste as he waved a languid hand toward O'Neill, "coverall."

O'Neill closed his eyes and counted to ten. "What do I need to do to get this job? I don't have enough credit to pay for a shuttle dirtside, so I need to work."

» «

VANTI LAUGHED SO HARD she must have nearly wet herself. "Oh, my gawd! You— you—!" She leaned against the wall, tears running down her face.

O'Neill glared. With the new platinum blond, high-n-tight, flat-top cut, his nose looked sharper and his eyes deeper set. "I'm not worried about the hair—it'll grow. I'm more concerned about my dignity. I was barely able to talk him out of green skin and blue eyes!" He unzipped his coverall and dropped the sleeves off his arms.

Vanti started howling again. "He made you wear an electric blue skin suit? Oh, my gawd! You should sue for sexual harassment!" She fell onto the futon, wrapping her arms around her middle as she wailed with laughter. The cloud of dust caught in her throat and her laughter became a coughing fit.

O'Neill glared. "Tell me you learned something, so I can stop humiliating myself. If anyone had told me four years ago that I'd be sweeping up hair wearing something from a bad music vid, I'd have laughed myself silly."

"Well, I'm doing that now, so full circle." Vanti pulled herself together and sat up. "OK, here's what I've got. According to all the neighbors, Taban definitely has alternate income. The neighbors say very few clients frequent the place. The *Sprzężaj* collects protection money from everyone on the Level, and he pays just like everyone else. And he still has money to pay rent. That credit is coming from somewhere."

"So, you think he's our guy?" O'Neill grabbed a pair of shorts and a shirt from his bag and headed to the tiny bathroom.

"Don't jump the gun," Vanti said with a shake of her head. "I think he's worth checking out. I can't believe our first target would be the winner, can you? It's never that easy."

"Yeah, I guess you're right. I'm going to change into something actually comfortable."

"But you look so good in blue, Griz," Vanti called as he closed the bathroom door.

When he came back out, Vanti had laid dinner out on the tiny table. "Since you're the working half of this contract, I figured I should make dinner. Got some nice greens on Level 25."

"Is that farmers' market sanctioned?" O'Neill tossed his skin suit into the hammock and sat down at the table.

"We're not on black market duty, Griz, so don't ask." Vanti handed him a bowl. "And if you get it shut down, I will make you sorry."

The meal was good: rice, beans, sautéed greens, and a spicy sauce. "Where'd you learn to cook?" He chased the last bean around the bowl with spoon and scooped it into his mouth.

"I know how to find recipe vids and follow directions. Since it's all gone, I assume you liked it?" She stirred her own bowl and nibbled on a tiny bite.

"Yeah, it was great. I'm glad you didn't take the cover job after all, or I'd be cooking. We'd both be sorry."

THREE

THE NEXT FEW weeks followed the same pattern. O'Neill spent the day cleaning up in Doable Do. Every week, Taban insisted on changing his look, and he acquired four more brightly colored, shiny, form-fitting suits. The curses he uttered while getting dressed owed as much to his appearance as to the difficulty in getting into the skin-tight garb.

Meanwhile, Vanti snooped around the lower levels, shopping and asking questions. Locals were friendly but cautious around strangers, and she picked up little useful information. In the evenings, they picked a level and walked all the rings and radials, chatting with anyone who would engage.

Thursday night, they strolled through Level 17. Although it was "late" according to the station's arbitrary time clock most of the businesses stayed open. Keeping a business alive on the lower levels took a lot more than forty hours a week. They strolled the circumference of Ring E and turned out-station on Radial 3.

At the corner to D Ring, a large curly-haired man in stained clothing blocked their way. O'Neill urged Vanti around him, but the man stepped in front of them. Vanti dodged left, and O'Neill went right. Curly blocked O'Neill, and another equally large man stepped out of the shadows into Vanti's path.

"The *Księżna* invites you to join her for a late meal." The first man showed his teeth as if he'd been told to smile but would prefer to chew asteroids.

"The who invites us where?" Vanti asked, reaching slowly into her pocket.

She probably has a knife in there, O'Neill thought. He laid a hand on her arm. Not that Vanti would need a weapon to take these guys. O'Neill had sparred with her in many classes. He was proud to say he'd beaten her, once.

"The *Księżna*. She is the Duchess of the *Sprzężaj*. You may have heard of the *Sprzężaj?*" Curly gestured for them to follow the second man down D Ring. "Please, follow my *przyjaciel*."

Vanti and Ty exchanged looks and turned to follow. "Follow his satchel?" Vanti muttered. O'Neill shrugged.

"*Przyjaciel* means friend in Poelish." The man behind them leaned in close and lowered his voice conspiratorially. "We don't use names in front of outsiders. You understand."

"Where is Satchel taking us?" Vanti demanded.

The man ignored her. About halfway down the corridor, Satchel stopped, waving his holo-ring at a door marked "Maintenance." The door whooshed open, and Vanti and O'Neill exchanged another look. "Does Satchel work for the station?" Vanti asked. Satchel ignored her and stomped into the duct, ducking beneath the low-hanging conduits.

The narrow duct forced them to walk single file, so O'Neill let Vanti take the lead. If it came down to a fight, he was confident he could incapacitate one of their escorts, but he hoped it wouldn't come to that. Satchel turned again, and a door opened automatically as he approached. He ducked into the bot garage and they crowded in. With a grunt, Satchel popped open a panel and revealed a ladder.

"We'll climb down from here," he said, his voice high pitched and grating. It sounded odd coming from his massive form. "Level 11."

"Why don't we just take the float tubes?" O'Neill suggested. "We'd love to meet the Chensa."

"*Księżna*," Curly corrected, squeezing in behind them. Vanti climbed up on top of one of the cleaning bots to make more room. Curly shut the door with a flick to his holo-ring. "She prefers to keep this visit private."

"Private from whom?" O'Neill asked, but neither man answered.

Satchel swung onto the ladder and quickly dropped out of sight. Curly nodded at Vanti. "You're next."

"I'm not sure I can climb down six levels," Vanti said breathlessly. "That's a long way and I'm not that strong."

The man laughed, much louder and longer than necessary. "You'll be fine," he said, pointing at the hatch. Vanti shook her head but followed directions. "Your partner is very amusing," Curly told O'Neill.

"Yeah, so are you." He climbed in after Vanti.

"You know there are cams all over this station." Vanti's voice carried up the shaft. "Anyone with access to the feeds will know where we are."

"Save it for the duchess," O'Neill hissed down at her.

"Listen to your friend," Curly said. "He's a smart man, even if he doesn't look like one."

By the time they reached Level 11, O'Neill's biceps burned and sweat beaded on his forehead. He swiped a hand over his face and through his hair. This week it was tawny, shoulder-length waves. The long strands stuck to his neck and cheeks. Once this assignment was over, he vowed he'd never have long hair again.

Satchel led them out of another bot closet and through the ducts to a narrow door made of synth wood. Unlike the usual duct doors, this one opened on hinges instead of an automated sliding mechanism. Clearly it had been retrofitted, which meant the compartment on the other side had not originally been connected to the ducts. He signaled Vanti in finger code: "Unknown adversary/be ready."

Vanti rolled her eyes and gave him the "You think?" sign. At least that's what he assumed that gesture meant.

Satchel knocked and scratched at the door in a complex pattern. A few seconds later, it opened into a dark room. Satchel stepped aside, and Curly prodded Vanti and O'Neill through. "Good luck," Curly said, shutting them into the dark.

A light flared overhead. O'Neill sidestepped away from the door and whirled in one quick motion. Out of the corner of his eye, he saw Vanti do the same, in the opposite direction. They stood there, half crouched, ready for action.

"Bravo! You are like dancers, perfectly in step." A tiny old woman sat in a large throne on a raised step on the far side of the room. She wore an orange cardigan over a black shirt, and a fluffy pink blanket covered her legs. As they straightened, she raised a bottle of beer in salute and took a swig.

"You are the Chensa?" Vanti asked.

"*Księżna*," the old woman corrected. Then she shrugged. "It's hard to pronounce if you don't speak the language."

"Do you speak the language? I thought Ancient Earth languages were all dead." Vanti strolled across the room and dropped into one of the chairs grouped around a table near the throne. O'Neill admired her cool.

The woman laughed. "They are dead, but that doesn't mean no one speaks them. I learned Poelish at my mother's knee. Well, at least a few words of it. Enough chit-chat. Tell me why two security agents are pretending to be lower-lev drones."

"How—What do you mean?" O'Neill's voice cracked a little. With that old woman staring down at him, he felt fifteen instead of twenty-five.

"Don't bother," Vanti said, briskly. "The Poelish mafia obviously has people embedded in SK'Corp. She probably knows our ID numbers and favorite foods."

The *Księżna* shrugged. "You are Tiberius O'Neill y Mendoza bin Tariq e Reynolds and Lindsay Fioravanti Rodriguez-Chang y Buccafurni, commonly known as Vanti. I could get your ID numbers, of course. But favorite foods are harder. I'd say pizza," she pointed at O'Neill, then tilted her head, staring at Vanti, "*Krehm Broolay?*"

Vanti's lips quirked. "Close enough. We're investigating a murder."

"The Chair? Good riddance, I'd say." The *Księżna* flipped the blanket aside and stood. She wore tight denim pants and boots with sparkly stones embedded in swirling patterns. Although her face looked to be about ninety years old, she had the body of a much younger woman. Or one who'd had all the top-grade esthetic mods. "But the 'how' is intriguing. What do your scientists say?"

"Nanobots," Vanti said.

"Vanti!" O'Neill was stunned at her lack of discretion.

Vanti shook her head. "She already knows. I think she can help us, but she's only going to do that if we help her. And the first step to making that kind of mutually beneficial agreement is establishing trust."

"Listen to your partner, young man." The *Księżna* stepped down from the dais. "The *Sprzężaj* does not tolerate murder on our station." She pinned him with her iron gaze. "We also will not tolerate interference. If you don't choose to help us, we will remove you from the situation."

"What do you mean, 'remove'?" O'Neill said with a gulp.

"Our specialty," she said with a smile. "We are experts at making people disappear. Don't worry, we don't kill anyone." She held up a hand, warding off such an idea. "We just remove you from the station."

"If that's not a euphemism for killing, I don't know what you mean," O'Neill said.

Vanti looked up. "Exactly what she said. I've heard of the *Sprzężaj*--they relocate people--sometimes willingly, sometimes not. But if you don't want to end up penniless and without ID or holo-ring, in a swamp on Grissom, I suggest we cooperate." She looked up at the older woman. "We think he was injected two to three days before he died, then the nanobots were activated remotely. One of our sources pointed us to Taban as a possible source."

The *Księżna* pulled two more bottles of beer from a small fridge behind the throne and handed them to Vanti and O'Neill. "My sources also suggest Taban might be involved. We know he supplies unlicensed nanobots to anyone willing to pay. But he isn't the killer." She plopped down in another chair and waved at the third. "Have a seat, Agent O'Neill. We have much to discuss."

FOUR

O'NEILL PEERED through the open bathroom door at Vanti's reflection in the mirror. Her modded blond hair stuck out in two tails from each side of her head. She caught his eye and gave him a glare. O'Neill clamped down on a laugh and turned away.

"What are you laughing at?" Vanti straightened her short, flowered skirt and tucked in her white, puffy-sleeve blouse. "This Poelish costume is ridiculous, but not as stupid as that." She waved a hand at him, encompassing his entire body.

Which was currently encased in lime green StretchTight SkinSuit. O'Neill held up his hands in surrender. "I know, but if I don't laugh, I'll cry. It's been two weeks since we started working with the *Księżna*. We need a break soon, or I might just grab a pair of shears and go on a wild hair-hacking rampage. I'll start with these stupid green dreadlocks."

"I might skewer someone with a chopstick first. And it might be you, if you keep leaving your dirty clothes lying around." She slipped the toe of her ankle-high station boot under a discarded shirt and deftly kicked it at his head.

He laughed and grabbed the shirt as it sailed at his face. He spun and tossed it into the basket behind the futon. "Two!" Then he grabbed a protein bar and tossed it to her. "We gotta move."

They headed down the hall toward the float tubes. "You know, the *Księżna* claims to be some kind of Poelish expert, but I'm pretty sure chopsticks weren't used in Poelville. My great grandmother was Shinese, and she used chopsticks. Shina was half-way around the Earth from Poelville." Vanti ripped open her breakfast and took a bite.

O'Neill shrugged. "I'm not telling her. I don't want to end up in a desert on Armstrong with medically induced amnesia. I'll see you after work. It's your turn to get dinner."

Vanti leaned in and kissed him on the cheek. "Bye darling—no, that is not going to work. One of these days I'll come up with a pet name I can live with." With a finger wave, she stepped into the float tube. O'Neill followed a moment later, exiting on Level 5 to endure another sweaty, humiliating day at Doable Do.

He set the mini-vacu-bot to run each time Moirrey finished with a client. Then he wiped down all the surfaces, and stacked towels and equipment at each station according to the day's schedule. He finished with time to kill before the shop opened. None of the stylists had arrived, so he set an alert on the door and let himself through the storage area and into the business office in the back.

He'd been in here several times over the past month and found nothing. He'd used a hacking program written by the code jockeys upstairs to break into Taban's accounts, but they showed only legitimate purchases and expenses. Either Taban was clean—unlikely according to the *Księżna*—or he was extremely careful.

He wandered around the room, hoping something would just jump out at him. Nothing out of the ordinary. No secret safe hidden behind a picture, no handwritten ledgers detailing sales of contraband. No secret passageways behind a bookshelf.

The front door alert pinged. A quick look around confirmed the only place to hide was under the desk. If Taban came in and found him hiding, he'd be screwed. He moved to the door and out into the supply room.

"...shouldn't even let you into the shop this late! Moirrey and that stupid assistant of hers will be here any minute," Taban said.

"We will only be two minutes," a scratchy voice replied. "But I must have the product today. Now." Even through the poor-quality audio feed, O'Neill could hear the menace in the voice. This could be the break he'd been waiting for. He ducked behind the last row of shelves, hoping the "product" wasn't hidden here between the hair color and skin-toners.

The door swished open, and O'Neill peeked between the boxes and cartons, cursing himself for not installing surveillance cams when he first arrived. He'd thought about it, but figured he could have the techies upstairs review station surveillance for him. Now he realized Taban would have disabled or spoofed any station cams in the shop if he was doing illegal business. Rookie mistake!

Taban and a tall woman with dark hair and startling white skin walked in. Taban wore a drab robe which he threw off as soon as the door closed. Underneath, he sported his usual flamboyantly colored StretchTight Skin-Suit. Today his hair was red and curly, with flowers woven in. The woman wore a standard SK2 station coverall, with an ops badge on the chest.

O'Neill used his holo-ring to snap a couple pictures. Even if the station cams were useless, he should have enough pics to run an ID program. As the two moved closer to his end of the room, he crouched down behind the shelves, wishing his own clothing was less colorful.

"Here it is," Taban said from the other side of the box O'Neill hid behind. Heart pounding and palms sweating, O'Neill held his breath. The other man was so close.

"No one ever uses BodySkuplt anymore, so it's a perfect place to keep the product."

"I don't care where you keep it." The woman's scratchy voice grated over O'Neill's spine, sending shivers through his body. "Just give it to me." Clicking and whirring noises drifted through the room. "Perfect, this checks out. And you've given me five doses as requested."

"I'm not giving you anything," Taban said pleasantly. "I'm selling you five doses. Fifty-three hundred credits. Each."

"Of course," the woman replied, "but I don't need five doses. I only need four. I'll leave this one with you."

Taban shrieked. Something slammed against the shelf, raining boxes, packages and bottles down on O'Neill's head. It slammed again, and the shelf crashed down, pinning O'Neill beneath.

"What are you doing? I'm your only source. You need me!" Taban's voice went from begging to demanding.

"I needed you." The gravelly voice stressed the past tense. "But I don't need you anymore. Once this job is finished, I'll disappear. And I don't need to leave any evidence behind."

"No!" Taban called, but the door swooshed open and the woman was gone.

O'Neill shoved against the shelf, but it wouldn't move. The shelf against the back wall had prevented it from crushing him, leaving a narrow triangle of space. He flicked his holo-ring. "Vanti, find this woman. She just left the Doable Do. I don't know where she's headed, but she's our target." He flicked the pictures to her and signed off before she could reply.

"Who's there?" Taban cried.

"It's me, Mick." He pushed broken bottles and equipment away, trying to clear a path to the end of the shelf. "What did she do to you?"

"She injected me with the nanobots!" He cried. "She's going to kill me!"

"Is there any way to stop the process?" O'Neill asked, inching his way forward.

"No!" Taban wailed. "She's going to kill me! All she has to do is send the command, and the nanobots will stop my heart."

Karma's a bitch, isn't it? O'Neill thought. "Who is she? Who is her target?"

"I don't know! We don't exchange names in this kind of business! And I don't want to know what she's going to do with the product. You have to help me!" The shelf shook. O'Neill looked up between the shelves and saw Taban slumped against the angled metal.

"If you get off the shelf, I can get out and help you," O'Neill said, trying to sound reasonable.

"No one can help me!" Taban's cry wavered up into a keen.

O'Neill pushed his shoulder against the shelf and shoved up with his legs as hard and fast as he could. Taban and the shelf jolted, and the rest of the contents fell to the floor. O'Neill shoved again, and Taban stumbled across the aisle to the other shelf. O'Neill threw the shelf off and staggered out of the tumbled piles of destroyed beauty products. He ran to Taban and grabbed his shoulders. "Tell me what you know about that woman. How did she find you? What else have you sold her? Quickly, before it's too late!"

Taban's face turned gray and he began sweating. A hand went to his throat. "BodySkulpt," he whispered. His eyes rolled back, and he collapsed.

O'Neill dropped down beside him, feeling for a pulse. Nothing. He activated a med alert on his holo-ring and started resuscitation.

Medical took five minutes to arrive. The hospital was on Level 45, a trip that should take little more than sixty seconds. But emergencies on the lower levels apparently rated a less speedy response. As soon as the med techs arrived, O'Neill called Vanti.

"Where are you?" he demanded.

"I'm in the float tube. I called Security Command. They followed your perp via vid. They got her leaving the Doable Do. She took the float tube, but they spotted her on Level 63. She went into an office in B Ring. I'm on my way there, now."

"Wait for backup! Are they sending someone?"

"Yes, mother, I'm waiting. I'm on 63 now. I'll flip you the body cam feed." A vid popped up on O'Neill's holo. Vanti's breathing rasped through the feed as she ran down Radial 4. She pounded down the corridor and skidded around the corner at B Ring. She took a position outside compartment 26, her back against the wall.

"ETA?" O'Neill asked. He dragged his eyes away from the holo and focused on the mess around him. Med techs worked on Taban, but their movements had slowed, as if they knew it was too late. The shelf that had fallen on O'Neill lay tilted against the back wall, the contents scattered across the floor.

"Command says they're on the level now," Vanti replied. She turned back the way she'd come, as five armored security agents ran up the hallway. They took up positions, had Ops pop the door and streamed into the compartment.

"Clear! Clear! Clear!" Vanti stepped into the room.

"Where is she?" O'Neill demanded.

Vanti turned slowly, so he could see the whole room. "She's gone."

FIVE

PEOPLE SPILLED out of the Happy Poel in the usual lunchtime rush. O'Neill pushed between bodies, ignoring the strange looks and snickers his clothing inspired. Once he got through the door, the crowd thinned, as most of them were queued up at the to go line.

He took a seat in the corner of the room, at one of the few empty tables. The *Księżna* dozed in a throne against the back wall. O'Neill did a double take. That throne appeared to be a twin to the one she'd been sitting in when they first met. She took her "duchess" title seriously. Vanti had warned him to never approach the *Księżna* when she was sleeping, so he ordered a beer and waited.

The crowd flowed around him, dwindling as lunchtime ended, and folks headed back to work. Finally, Vanti stepped out of the kitchen. Her blonde hair hung limply on either side of her head, and a sheen covered her face. She wiped her hands on a towel, threw it down on the counter, and crossed to O'Neill's table.

"Let's go talk to her," she said, jerking her head at the *Księżna*.

"I thought we had to wait until she wakes up." O'Neill stood and followed Vanti across the room.

"She's awake. She's playing Galactic Aviator on a neural link." Vanti pointed at a tiny red light on the throne. "The light turns green so Ye'an knows when she's 'receiving.' She gets pissed if you interrupt her. But she called you here, so she'll see us."

The *Księżna's* eyes opened, and the tiny light turned green. "I'm sure you von't tell anyvon our leetle secret," she said, pointing at the tiny light. "Seet here." She waved at two low stools that sat on the dais next to her throne.

O'Neill gave Vanti a questioning look, but she just sat down. He followed her lead. A faint hum and vibration started, and the dais turned slowly, rotating through the wall. Seconds later, they found themselves in the same room where they'd visited the *Księżna* the first time.

"Nifty," O'Neill said. "What's up with the accent?"

The *Księżna* shrugged. "It's expected. You can't be duchess of the Poelish mafia if you sound like a station rat." All trace of the accent was gone.

"Another thing," O'Neill said. He was in a grumpy mood and didn't care if the duchess knew it. "The first time we came here, you insisted we climb down an access shaft to avoid notice. Seems to me sitting on a turning platform in front of a full restaurant is hardly stealthy."

"Now that 'Lisa' is working here, your visit is feasible. And it is not unusual for me to summon the partners of new employees for a private visit. You can get away with a lot when you're the *Księżna*. As to the rotating dais—I like a little drama. But now," she threw off the blanket and stood, "we have work to do."

"What work?" O'Neill crossed his arms and stayed stubbornly in his seat. "I basically witnessed a murder, didn't manage to stop it, and the killer got away. Forensics didn't find any more BodySkulpt boxes, so we don't even have any hard evidence."

"Stop griping, Griz." Vanti stood. "It was my fault she got away, not yours." She turned toward the *Księżna*. "What's your plan?"

The *Księżna* moved toward the synth wood door. "We're going up to 63 to check out the compartment she disappeared from."

O'Neill stared at the old woman in disbelief. "No offense, but how's that going to work? I'm not sure I can climb fifty plus levels. I have a hard time believing you can."

The woman grinned. "First, we aren't climbing. Second, I'm not as ancient as I look." She slid her fingers up into her hairline and did something. As they watched, her face changed. Her cheeks filled in, her eyes brightened, her wrinkles slowly smoothed out. In sixty seconds, her apparent age went from ninety to forty. Even her hair looked fuller.

"How did you do that?" Vanti breathed.

She pulled back her white hair, revealing a series of tiny silver dots along her hairline. "Programmable visual disruption field. It lays the image of an older woman over my own face." Her fingers twitched in her hairline again, and the wrinkled crone reappeared. "If you look closely, you can see that the wrinkles aren't real. But no one gets that close to the *Księżna*."

"If I, what? Put it on? Had one installed? Whatever. If I had one of these, would I look like you?" Vanti leaned in close to inspect the *Księżna's* face.

"Installed. The nodes are implanted under the skin and draw power from my body. No, you would look like an older version of you."

O'Neill realized his mouth was hanging open and shut it. Then he opened it again to ask, "Why?"

"Continuity. It allows the *Księżna* to reign for a long time. I'm actually the third woman to hold this position in the last twenty years. My mother and sister were *Księżna* before me, but they've since retired. We look a lot alike. Once you add the PVD field, we're almost indistinguishable."

Vanti asked, "Are they still here on SK2?"

The *Księżna* turned back to Vanti. "My sister, Marcella, is still here. She works in another part of the station. She filled in as *Księżna* last week when I went dirtside for vacation. I enjoy betting on the dog races. Come." And with that, she led the way out the door.

They went back to the bot closet Curly and Satchel had brought them through. The *Księżna* unlocked a cabinet. She pulled out a flat panel with two notches cut in one side. "Here, hold this." She shoved it at O'Neill. Then she opened the access panel to the ladder shaft. "Now stick it in here."

O'Neill hesitated. "Why are you helping us?" He waved off her obvious answer. "I know you don't want murder on the station. But you've just shared your identity with us. Doesn't that make us dangerous to you? Why would you do that?"

The woman sighed. "Honestly? Being the *Księżna* kind of sucks. I mean, I'm stuck on that stupid throne all day. If I turn off the PVD, I can go out, but I still have to maintain a distance from most people. Since you're sec agents, I'm pretty sure you two aren't going to try to blackmail or out me."

She shrugged again. "I guess I'm bored. Besides, if you betray me, I'll deny everything and make you disappear." She smiled and turned back to the ladder shaft.

The notches in the panel fit over the side rails of the ladder. The *Księżna* flicked a switch on the panel and stepped up onto it. "Come on. And while I have the PVD deactivated, call me Sonia."

Vanti and O'Neill climbed onto the flimsy looking platform. It vibrated quietly, then started moving up the shaft. "I can't believe those goons made us climb down the ladder!" Vanti said.

"I don't let them use the lift panel," Sonia said. "They need to stay in shape."

It took about ten minutes to get up to Level 63. They climbed out through the access hatch, and O'Neill removed the lift panel at Sonia's request. "Stash it behind that bot," Sonia pointed across the bot closet. O'Neill stuck the panel behind the bot, and Sonia stuck a note on the bot, "Broken, don't move." She smiled, moving toward the door. "Sometimes low tech is best."

"Hang on," Vanti said. "That woman disappeared from an internal compartment. That means there's an access other than the public corridors. This station is a standard build on every level. So, we should be able to reach that access from here, just like we can reach your restaurant from the bot closet." She pointed downward.

O'Neill snapped his fingers. "Good call! Sonia, do you have access to station schematics?"

Sonia nodded and flicked her holo-ring. She flipped through a series of screens, then popped one open. "Here's Level 63. It looks like there should be a duct from here to the compartment, right through there." She pointed at another bot. "There's an access behind that bot."

O'Neill dragged the bot out of the way and ducked down into the space behind it. "There's a panel here, but it's activated by the bot. Can you turn it on?"

Vanti fiddled with the bot for a few minutes. "Nope, can't turn it on. You're going to have to do it manually."

"Are there any tools here?" O'Neill poked his head back out.

Sonia dug through a couple cabinets, then handed him a device. "Try this."

"Perfect!" O'Neill popped the panel open. "We'll have to crawl."

"No," said Sonia. She pitched the level schematic to his holo-ring. "You can crawl. Vanti and I will go through the public corridors and meet you there."

"Thanks a lot," O'Neill muttered, but they were already gone. He flipped on the glow feature of his holo and crawled into the duct. The cleaning bots used these ducts to reach the compartments in the level, and they were only as tall as the bots required. The ducts they'd used down on Level 11 must have been modified to allow more comfortable access for the *Sprzężaj*.

O'Neill tried crawling. He tried scooting on his butt. He tried duck walking. None of them were comfortable. By the time he reached a space which the schematic showed backed up on the compartment, he was sweating, and his knees ached.

The duct looked exactly the same here. No obvious doors or panels. He pounded on the duct wall. All that did was make his ears ring. He flicked his holo-ring and called Vanti. A tiny holo of her popped up in his palm. "I'm here--how do I get out?"

She shrugged. "We don't see any obvious accesses here."

"Ugh. I don't want to crawl all the way back." He massaged his lower back. "Maybe I'll just sleep here tonight."

He crawled a little further and finally found a panel. Using the tool Sonia had given him, he opened it and stepped out into a small closet. He groaned, slowly straightening. "Next time, you get to crawl through the ducts."

"Where are you?" Vanti asked.

"Not sure." He climbed over discarded shoes, ducked through a rack of clothing, and opened the door.

An ear-piercing scream rang through the room, just before a vase slammed into his shoulder.

O'NEILL FLUNG UP HIS HANDS. "Stop! I'm a security agent! I won't hurt you!" The vase dropped to the floor, bouncing once.

A little girl stood across the room, glass picture frame clutched in her hand. "What are you doing in our closet?" she shrieked.

"Vanti, help me out here," he muttered. No response. "I'm just, uh, checking security on the station. There's a bot access in the closet that needs to be locked. I'll open a maintenance ticket on it."

The girl's eyes narrowed. "If you're a sec agent? Where's your badge?"

He flicked his holo-ring and pulled up his credentials. Stepping forward, he held out his hand, so she could see the file in his palm. She raised the frame a few centimeters, and he froze. That vase had hurt, and this frame looked even heavier. He flicked the file toward the girl.

She caught the file on her own holo and looked at it. "Where's your uniform?" She carefully set the frame down on a table.

"I'm undercover. People get nervous if they see a sec agent wandering around looking at things, so we do our checks in plain clothes. I'm Ty."

"I'm Izzy. I like your hair." She reached out and touched one of his dreadlocks. "My mom makes me comb mine."

"Where are you?" Vanti's voice echoed through his ear.

"Oh, now you can hear me. It's just good luck I wasn't permanently impaired by a vase thrown by a twelve-year-old."

"You think I'm twelve?" The girl dissolved into giggles. "I'm six."

"Even better. A six-year-old almost brained me."

She giggled even harder. "I didn't almost brain you. That vase is Rub*er. It doesn't hurt." She picked up the vase and squished it in her hand, then bounced it off her head.

"Gimme that!" O'Neill grabbed the vase, squeezing it experimentally. "Well, I'll be an alien's mutt. It didn't feel like Rub*er when it hit me. The frame, too?"

"Course. My mom doesn't let us have breakable stuff. The baby might hurt hi'self." She pointed to a playpen in the corner. Fortunately, it was empty.

"Could we please get back on task?" Vanti's voice ratcheted up a couple notes. "Is this child's mother anywhere nearby? We need to question her about that duct. And--."

The sound of crackling electricity was the last thing O'Neill heard.

» «

"--BUT you won't press charges?" The whining tone grated on O'Neill's nerves.

"I think we can overlook the incident." Vanti's voice came from far away. "Your stunner is illegal, but Agent O'Neill entered your compartment without advanced notice or proper identification."

"I had proper ID." O'Neill coughed and tried again. "I showed the girl-- Izzy."

"Izzy is six, and you were already in my compartment when you showed it to her!" A frazzled looking woman in an expensive suit loomed over him. O'Neill sat up.

"He's a sec agent, and we have the right to inspect every square centimeter of this station!" Vanti rounded on the woman. "You attacked a member of an active security detail. We could have you sent dirtside in a heartbeat!"

The woman deflated. "No! Don't do that! Izzy's father is down there."

"The planet isn't big enough for both of you?" O'Neill asked, climbing slowly to his feet. He looked around the room. "Where's Sonia?"

Vanti gave a tiny head shake and turned back to the woman. "Did anyone come through this compartment earlier today?"

"Would I have left my daughter alone if someone had?" The woman dropped onto the child-sized bed. She flicked her holo-ring and pulled up surveillance footage. "I'll throw you the nanny cam recording."

"Nanny cam?! Have you been spying on me?" The little girl stared at her mother, outraged. "You said I was old enough to stay home alone!"

"I don't watch it, Stardust! I promise I don't. It's just in case."

O'Neill tuned out the arguing voices and focused on the vid. "There she is."

The mother's voice cut off, mid word. She watched, mouth open, as the woman in the image strolled across Izzy's room and stepped into the closet.

"She could be anywhere." Vanti rubbed the back of her neck. "Well, I guess that's all we need to see here. Ma'am, I'm going to have to confiscate your stunner as evidence."

The woman pulled the child toward her. "You can have it. But I need a safe place to stay. We can't live here!"

O'Neill waved a hand at her. "I'll put in a maintenance ticket to have the access hatch sealed. Go stay with friends for a few days. They'll let you know when it's done."

They left the woman frantically calling friends in search of a temporary home. "Why doesn't she just lock the closet?" Vanti led the way down the hall to the next compartment and jerked a thumb at the door. "Sonia's inside."

"We still don't know how this woman--"

"Let's call her TDC," Vanti interrupted. "Tall, dark and creepy."

O'Neill snorted. "Fine. We don't know how TDC got from 26 to Izzy's compartment."

"Yes, we do." Sonia stood inside the single room, holding the discarded coverall.

"Care to share that information, Sonia?" O'Neill grated out.

Sonia reached out and touched a seemingly blank spot on the wall. The wall shimmered, as if a wave of heat flowed over it, and then a seam appeared. A seam around a standard sized door. "Similar technology to my PVD," she said, "I would open this, but I'm afraid Izzy would take out my eye with that picture frame."

They went around and knocked on the front door. Izzy's mother opened it, frowning at them. Sonia strode to a wall hanging, lifted it up, and fumbled for the controls. The door appeared.

"That hanging was there when I moved in," Izzy's mother cried. "I never looked behind it."

Vanti snorted. "Then you might want to check behind that bookshelf." She winked at Izzy as they left.

Back in the bot closet, O'Neill turned to the women. "Now what? We know TDC took four doses of lethal nanobots. Then she came up here and disappeared through this bot duct. She could be anywhere in the station. The facial recognition program hasn't gotten any hits. She said she was going to use those doses and then disappear. The sec team hasn't found any more useful evidence in Taban's salon. We don't know who she is or what she wants. We don't even know if she was connected to the chair's death. Does that pretty much sum it all up?"

"Thanks, Griz, that was so helpful." Vanti paced the tiny room. "Why don't we focus on what we do know?"

"And what would that be?" He yanked the lift panel out from behind the bot and fitted it into place in the ladder shaft. Turning, he reached out a hand to Sonia to help her on. She gave him a grateful nod and stepped up. Vanti rolled her eyes and leapt lightly onto the platform. He followed.

As they started down the shaft, Vanti listed items on her fingers. "We know there are four more targets. These could be board members or someone else. We know the person behind all this—or at least one of them —is a woman."

"Hang on," O'Neill interrupted. "How do we know it's a woman? She looked female, but that can be faked. All we really have to go on is height and build. That can narrow down our field a little, but not much." He sighed.

"Fine. We're looking for an apparently female person, approximately 177 centimeters, and seventy to eighty kilograms in mass. We have a voice print, which SecTech can run through an all channel comparison. Forensics probably got some DNA at the salon. I'm going to recommend additional security on all board members and voice checks at all ports before passengers are allowed to embark."

O'Neill stared at his partner. "Wow. That's way more than I thought we had." He turned to the other woman. "What do you think, Sonia?"

The older woman started. "I'm not sure. I—nothing is working out as I expected. I guess we'll keep trying. Vanti's ideas are better than anything I can come up with."

They rode the rest of the way down in silence. In the bot closet, O'Neill put the lift panel away, then opened the door for Sonia. "We'll see you later, Sonia."

"No!" Sonia stopped dead in the doorway. "You must come back to the Happy Poel with me. If you don't, someone will suspect there is another exit from my compartment."

"I kind of assumed there was," Vanti said. "I mean, you don't really think people believe you spend all day and night in that tiny room behind the restaurant, do you?"

"They do believe it. That's one of the keys to the *Księżna* mystery. She runs the lower half of the station from the back of the restaurant."

"Whatever," O'Neill said. "I just want to get moving on these leads."

When they reached the synth wood door, O'Neill held it open for the two women.

Sonia climbed into the throne, spreading the blanket over her lap. She reactivated the PVD and gestured toward the two stools. Vanti sat on one, but O'Neill stood next to the throne. "Aren't you going to sit down?" Sonia asked, reaching toward her control panel.

"For what? That gentle ride? I'll stand." As the platform started turning, he lurched against Vanti, then grabbed the throne for balance. "Sorry about that, maybe I'd better sit."

The *Księżna* shook her head. "Men."

They bid the *Księżna* farewell and strode back out into the corridors.

"Ok, what was that all about?" Vanti demanded.

"What?" O'Neill feigned innocence.

"Not sitting down on the turntable?"

"Was it that obvious?" O'Neill grinned.

"Yes." She drew the word out then narrowed her eyes. "You made it obvious. On purpose. Why?"

"I want them to find the bug I placed on the throne." He stepped into the float tube and dropped out of sight. Vanti followed.

"Classic misdirection," Vanti said as she stepped out and joined him on the Level 3 concourse. "You planted another one somewhere else."

"If they find the obvious one, maybe they won't look for the second," he confirmed.

They grabbed takeout in the concourse then hurried back to their compartment.

"Here's the audio from the bug on the throne." He flipped the sound icon up, and a background noise from the restaurant hummed through the speaker. "Here's the bug patch I placed on Sonia's arm when I helped her up onto the float panel."

Vanti flipped up another icon. "And here's the one I put on her neck when we were looking for the access panel in compartment 26. And the one on her boot. And the one under my stool at the restaurant." She flicked up two more icons.

"A bit of overkill, don't you think?" O'Neill opened the thermal pack and handed a steaming bowl of noodles to Vanti.

"Didn't realize you were setting some, too," she replied, getting utensils out of a drawer. "Fork or chopsticks?"

"Fork," O'Neill answered. "I still can't manage those things. Do your bug patches have locators on them?"

"Of course." She pulled up another screen and threw it over the audio icons. The station schematic opened, and all five icons stacked atop one another in the compartment labeled Happy Poel. "Either they haven't noticed any of them, or Sonia hasn't moved."

By the time they'd finished dinner, the bugs on the throne and the stool had been located and disabled. Just before the second disappeared from their holo, a deep voice growled. "No one spies on the *Sprzężaj*. You're lucky the *Księżna* likes you."

"You're a good boy Ye'an," the *Księżna's* voice rang through the speakers.

"I must rest now." The trackers rotated on the dais, and then all three moved through the door.

"Where do you think she's going?" O'Neill said, getting up to order some dessert through the AutoKich'n.

"I don't know. She was shaken by something in that compartment. Did you notice how she went from focused and helpful to vague and helpless?" Vanti chased the last chic'n fragment around her bowl with the chopsticks.

O'Neill thought back. She'd been holding that discarded coverall. "Sec-Tech must have cleared that compartment, right?" He pulled open the report. They'd done standard recordings and scans. When they were done, everything in that room could be recreated in the SecTech holo-stage. Well, everything except the hidden door. "How is it we don't know anything about these PVDs?"

Vanti rubbed a hand over her face. "I was wondering that, too. We're supposed to have the best tech out there. Maybe it's classified?" She opened a database and typed in a query. "Nothing."

"Could it have been invented by the *Sprzężaj*? Do they have an R and D department?" He stuck a spoon into his chocolate pudding.

"That smells really good," Vanti said, her eyebrows drawn down in surprise.

"You can't have any." O'Neill pulled the bowl close. "It's AutoKich'n food, and you don't eat that."

"Come on, let me try it! Then you can say 'I told you so.' Just one bite?" She smiled winningly.

"Fine, but get your own spoon." He turned back to the data and tried another query. "Look at this! There is a record of a similar sounding research. It was done here on station, and eventually abandoned for lack of results. Guess who the researcher was?"

Vanti leaned in close, peering over his shoulder. Her spoon fell to the table. "Marcella Krzyzewski Kolikowski. What do you want to bet that's Sonia's sister? And that her research wasn't a dead end, but rather co-opted for the *Sprzężaj*?" She clinked her spoon against his in triumph, and they both dug into the pudding.

"Blaargh!" Vanti jumped out of her seat and lunged to the sink. She stuck her head under the faucet and poured water over her tongue. O'Neil dove for the bathroom, spitting into the toilet, then swishing cup after cup of water in his mouth.

"What was that?" Vanti finally turned off the water and swiped at her wet shirt with a towel.

O'Neill shrugged and spit out a mouthful of SuperMint Freshener. "It was supposed to be chocolate pudding. I guess maybe you have a point about cheap AutoKich'n food."

She dumped the pudding bowl into the AutoKich'n and hit recycle. "So that explains Sonia's sudden change in attitude. Once she saw that PVD in compartment 26, she realized Marcella, or someone else in the *Sprzężaj* must be involved. I'm kind of surprised she showed it to us at all. Where is she now?"

They looked at the holo. The three audio icons showed Sonia in Cargo Bay H. "What do you supposed she's doing there?" O'Neill pulled on station shoes and grabbed his tool pack.

"I'll bet she's meeting Marcella." Vanti slung a sleek belt around her hips and checked the hidden pockets. Then she grabbed her tranq gun—perfect for the confined spaces on station. "You got the audio routed to your aural implant?"

"Of course," O'Neill replied with a tinge of disgust. Really, you'd think he was a cadet on his first mission, and Vanti a seasoned veteran. "I aced the same training sims you did," he reminded her. "With all this talk of betting, you're starting to sound like Sonia and her dog races."

SEVEN

THEY JOGGED up the corridor and out onto the concourse. Heavy crowds clogged the open spaces—a concert was scheduled to start in twenty minutes. Vanti and O'Neill pushed, squirmed, and threatened their way to the float tubes, then bounced up to Level 36. While passengers boarded interstellar cruisers through the scenic greenhouses on Level 40, walking along plasglass walled access bridges, cargo and crew accessed the ships via the warehouses on Levels 36 and 37. Windowless cargo tubes slanted up to deliver consumables, cargo, and relief crew to the lower levels of the ships.

The cargo levels were off-limits to most station personnel, but Vanti and O'Neill's sec agent IDs granted them access. They didn't bother to wonder how Sonia got in--she obviously had run of the station. The float tubes dumped them out in a caged area about nine meters square. O'Neill triggered the gate lock.

"Should we call for backup?" Vanti asked as they weaved through the massive stacks of cargo. Loader bots whizzed by, bearing crates, totes, and pallets of shrink-wrapped goods. She pointed out the thick yellow lines on the ground. "I think we need to stay between these."

Another bot zipped by, bare centimeters outside the yellow line, reinforcing her point. "I want to know what's going on first," O'Neill answered, pointing at a sign that read Bays H, I, J with a bright arrow beneath. "Sonia trusted us, so let's give her the benefit of the doubt."

They followed the signs for bay H, staying between the lines which protected them from the speeding bots. Their path ended with a red slash across the walkway. A bright red, flashing, holographic stop sign popped up before them. After a few seconds, the sign turned green, and a voice told them to proceed. The second they crossed a matching red line, bots began whizzing past behind them.

Traffic decreased as they approached bay H. "I've gotten access to the station schedules," Vanti said, as they jogged along between the yellow lines. "There's no ship in bay H."

"What are you doing?" A familiar voice demanded. Vanti and O'Neill stopped dead in their tracks, looking wildly around the warehouse. The workaholic bots skittered on, but no one else was visible.

"I'm doing what needs to be done," replied an eerily similar voice.

Vanti tapped her ear, and whispered, "Sonia." Of course. The audio links were live, and someone else must have joined the *Księżna*. O'Neill's aural implant pinged, with Vanti's ring tone. "It looks like they're in the main cargo bay." Vanti's voice echoed weirdly both through the air and in his implant. "You go in through the control booth, and I'll go through the crew access. There's a hatch to the main bay."

"Roger." O'Neill ran to the control booth door and tapped in his sec authorization. After a brief second, the door cycled open. The booth was a long narrow room with windows along one side looking out into the cargo bay. A control panel with several workstations ran the length of the room, so human cargo masters could monitor and direct loading. At the far end, a door led into the cargo bay.

"What do you mean by that?" Sonia demanded.

"Those top-levs will suck us dry," the other woman said. "They rob us of our livelihood and treat us as slaves."

O'Neill ducked low and ran to the far end of the room. The door whispered open at his command, and he stepped into the huge, cold space.

"You'll get no argument from me," Sonia replied, "but that's no justification for murder."

O'Neill, shielded by a huge cargo lifter, risked a look out into the bay.

Sonia and a woman who looked enough like her to be her twin stood in the center of the bay. Marcella looked nothing like the woman who had killed Taban, though. Were there others involved?

"How can we break free if not by force?" She paced back and forth, her gestures wild and forceful. "They are strangling us! Even the *Sprzężaj* is crippled by their grip!"

"Murder is not our way!" Sonia cried. "We, the *Sprzężaj*, have other means at our disposal."

"Right." The woman turned on Sonia with a harsh laugh. "Like you would dare to make a board member disappear. They would crush us all before we got him off station. That's why Smith had to be eliminated."

"Who are the other four targets?" Sonia asked. "Why only four?"

"How—who told you there are four more targets?" Marcella demanded.

"There was a witness at Taban's salon." Sonia shook her head slowly, as if disappointed in her sister. "You were too careless."

"I'm sure you can eliminate that witness for me."

"So, it was you? How did you change your appearance so much?" Sonia grabbed Marcella's arm.

Marcella smiled. "The PVD is much more flexible than you know. I've made a few improvements."

O'Neill straightened up. "Vanti, move in. She's said enough, and she's clearly working alone."

"Have you administered the other four doses yet?" Sonia asked, but Marcella heard something and spun toward O'Neill. With a shriek, she whipped a blaster out of her cloak and fired. The cargo lifter beside him shuddered and collapsed in a molten puddle.

O'Neill dodged across the room, weaving and bobbing. Marcella's blasts scorched the air in the bay. O'Neill yanked out his own blaster. With another shriek, she turned and ran.

Sonia raced after her sister. "Wait, Marcella, we can figure this out together!"

"Vanti, I'm taking fire. Where are you?" O'Neill demanded.

"I'm stuck in the freaking cargo air lock! The internal door won't open, and the crew access I came in through is jammed."

"They're headed your way." He pounded across the cargo bay, the two women several meters ahead. "Sonia, Marcella, there's nowhere to go!"

Marcella reached the cargo air lock, a huge door taking up most of the external wall. Generally, cargo was pushed into the airlock, which could be disconnected from the station's artificial gravity. Then bots moved the cargo through the lift tubes into the ships locked onto the station. For large loads, the outer airlock doors could be opened so station tugs could pull the cargo out to long-haul-shifters that were too large to dock at the station.

Marcella looked through the plasglas portal into the airlock and turned, baring her teeth. "Don't come any closer! I'll blow the outer lock, and your partner will be space dust!"

Sonia stopped, steps from her sister. "She knows how to do it," she said quietly. "She works here in cargo." She turned to the other woman. "You don't want to do this. There's no reason for you to kill again."

"Whose side are you on, Sonia?" Marcella demanded. "Would you choose these security agents over your own flesh and blood? Your own *siostra*?"

"You know the *Sprzężaj* always comes first. I would never put outsiders before family." Sonia took a step toward her sister.

Marcella put her hand over the control panel. "Don't!"

Vanti's white face peered through the plasglas, tight and wide-eyed. "Tranq her!" Her voice was loud and clear in O'Neill's ear.

"I can't," he muttered. "You have the tranq. I brought the blaster, and if I fire it that close to the cargo door, it could cause a serious breach. I'll see if I can move around to get a clear shot."

"Marcella, please, step away from the control panel." Sonia took another step toward her sister. "You don't want to hurt anyone. We can make this all go away. Just trust me." Sonia gestured toward O'Neill.

Vanti's eyes narrowed. "What is going on out there? It sounds like Sonia is planning to make you and me disappear. Take the shot!"

"No!" Marcella put her fingers on the control panel. "You can't fool me with your doublespeak. I taught you to do that! It's what makes us such good *Księżnas*! You are going to help those agents!"

"No! I told you, I'd never put them over *Sprzężaj*!" Sonia reached out.

Marcella's hands began shaking. "But you'd turn me over to the station to save the *Sprzężaj*!" She spit the words at her sister.

"Isn't that what you've taught me? To put the *Sprzężaj* first? To do whatever it takes to keep the *Sprzężaj* secure? Your actions are endangering all of us! When are you going to put the *Sprzężaj* first?"

"How dare you?! Everything I do is for the *Sprzężaj*! The board is choking all of us! The *Sprzężaj* won't survive if we don't break free. This—" she pulled something out of her pocket, "—is the key to survival."

Sonia leaped forward, clawing at the vial in Marcella's hand. O'Neill sprinted toward the struggling women. Sonia shrieked. Marcella cried out. They broke apart, and O'Neill grabbed Marcella's arm.

Sonia looked down at her arm, then up at her sister. "You—you've killed me!"

"No!" Marcella's face crumpled, and she reached out to the younger woman. "I didn't kill you! I didn't mean to inject you! You shouldn't have tried to take that away from me. It's not my fault."

"How long?" Sonia sat down against the cargo door.

O'Neill cuffed Marcella. "How long 'til what?" he asked.

Sonia gestured to her arm. "Until I'm dead?"

"Would someone get me out here?" Vanti called, hammering on the plasglas.

"We have a little situation out here," O'Neill growled. "You're fine in there."

"It's getting a little tight in here," she said, her voice tight.

"Tight? That airlock is huge! Are you claustrophobic?" O'Neill turned away from the door.

"You aren't going to die," Marcella said. "I'd have to activate the nanobots. I would never do that to you." Tears rolled down her face, and she pulled away from O'Neill to slide down the wall next to her sibling.

"So, I just live the rest of my life with this bomb inside me? You think that's OK?"

"Get me out of this airlock!" Vanti pounded harder on the plasglas.

O'Neill rubbed his forehead. Their voices pounded through his head. He turned on them. "Sonia, we'll talk to an esthetician. Someone else must know how to unprogram these things." He turned a little. "Marcella, you are going to a cell on Level 1. Vanti," he glared through the plasglas, "I'm calling maintenance, so chill out."

All three women looked at him for a second, then resumed their complaints, louder. O'Neill rubbed his temples praying for quiet.

EIGHT

VANTI ROLLED UP THE HAMMOCK, stuffing it into a sack. She tossed it to O'Neill. "You might need this in your fancy compartment up on 27. You probably can't afford furniture."

"You're one to talk about affording things. Maybe you should keep this. The dirtside pay scale is so low, you'll be lucky to afford an empty box." He tossed the bag back to her. "Are you sure you won't stay?"

"My life flashed before my eyes when I was stuck in that airlock. Repeatedly. All she had to do was push that button, and I'd have been sucked out into the void. There are a lot of risks to being a sec agent, but asphyxiation in outer space doesn't have to be one of them." She tossed the hammock back.

O'Neill pushed the StretchTight SkinSuits in with the hammock. "This is all going to security supply," he said with a wide smile. "With my promotion, I can afford some pretty nice furniture, thank you very much."

"I can't believe Don Said offered you a job in Board Security. I was the brains of this operation." She crammed the last of her personal belongings into a small tote bag.

"He offered it to you first. You said no."

"Yeah, I know." Vanti dropped her tote on the dusty futon. "Well, I guess

49

this is it, then. After four years of academy together, and one crazy assignment, we go our separate ways. I think I might actually miss you, Griz."

"Thanks, Vanti, I'll miss you too." O'Neill picked up her bag. "Come on, I'll walk you to the shuttle dock."

Vanti grabbed the bag and walked to the door. "No, it's better this way. I'll see you around, Griz. And whatever you do, don't eat the pudding."

And she was gone.

» «

VANTI AND O'NEILL are supporting characters in the *Space Janitor* series. If you enjoyed this story, check out the rest of the series on Amazon. Or turn the page for a sneak peek at The *Vacuum of Space*, the first book in the Space Janitor Series.

THE TROUBLE WITH TINSEL

ONE

Now I'm no Grinch, but I just want to go on record saying, "I hate tinsel." The garlands are bad enough—those fluffy ropes get caught in automatic doors and jam up the works. The long, stringy bits that are meant to resemble icicles are worse. Inevitably, someone will throw a handful, or twenty, into one of the float tubes, and we'll find the stuff all over the station, well into February.

But the door-sized, foil curtains of fringe are the worst. They're all the rage on SK2 this year. Fluttering drapes of bright, metallic tinsel wave across every corridor in the place. The loose reflective nature of those curtains confuses the bots. And when the two-meter-long strings break loose, they wrap around the gears inside the vacu-bots, sending them limping home to the garage.

Maybe I am a Grinch. Nothing stops up the works like Christmas. Sticky Kakuvian pine pitch on the floors, wrapping paper filling up the recycle chutes, drunken party-goers spewing in corners. The cleaning bots don't handle any of it well. Which means I have to. Handle it, that is.

My name is Triana Moore, and I'm a maintenance technician on Station Kelly-Kornienko. In other words, I'm a space janitor. Keeping the bots working is my bread and butter, and at Christmas time, that's no sleigh ride.

A FLASHING red icon catches my eye. I shove the last of a Toasty Pie into my mouth and roll my chair up to the console. Bot 23D is stuck. Running diagnostics tells me nothing, and the on-bot cam shows only clear corridor. I dispatch a repair drone and turn back to my Sweet Slurp.

A second flashing icon appears next the first. The repair bot has stopped about twenty meters from 23D. They're on cross corridors, so the two bots are not in line-of-sight, but a quick scan shows nothing near the repair bot. Now that's odd.

I tap into the vid feeds, but that intersection is dark. The cams are offline and can't be rebooted. My eyes narrow. This feels like hacking. But when I go into the operating system, there's no indication anyone else has been there. Hmmm.

I toggle the contact icon and tag the ops supervisor.

"Ops, al-Rashid-Thompson." The operations supervisor, "Rash," appears on the screen.

"Maintenance, Moore," I respond. "I got a couple bots up on Level 20 on the fritz. They aren't responding, and I can't get vid."

"Yeah, I noticed some cams were down. I was wondering when you were going to get around to fixing them." As he speaks, a banner flashes across my screen.

Level 20. Cams down.

"Hello! Space janitor, here. I don't fix cams, I just dust them." I lean in and swipe a sleeve over the cam I'm talking to. Rash waits until I lean back to roll his eyes. "But I'll take a look while I'm out there." I flick the banner, and the details pop up. They've been out for twenty minutes, so why didn't the alert come in right away? "Why didn't you tag repair?" Two can play the finger pointing game.

Rash holds up his hands. "I did. I'm just yanking your charging cable, Moore. We'll watch the store while you're out."

I sign off, forward the calls to Ops, and lock the MCC behind me. I bat the shiny green fringe of one of those zarking tinsel curtains out of my way and stride to the Level 2 concourse.

A thick airlock door separates the repair and maintenance section from the rest of Level 2. I wave my ring at the door, it cycles open. A wave of sounds slams into my eardrums. I fight my way through another tinsel curtain, this time red, and out into the crowded concourse.

Throngs of people crowd the open space, everyone with a cup, mug, or bottle in hand. Inflatable reindeer and a huge sparkly sleigh hang from the ceiling. A vendor sells something sticky-looking from a little cart on the far side of the space. A bar has been set up outside the small pub on my right, and a line of people wait in line for spiced wine. Fine, white confetti whirls through the space, floating on the wafts of circulating air. Christmas is still three days away, but when the holiday falls on a Monday, the party starts on Friday.

"Merry Christmas!" someone sings out, and a cheer goes up.

Scents of cinnamon, ginger, and nutmeg tease my nose and I sneeze. Inane Christmas music plays over the concourse speakers:

His little red spaceship shoots across the sky
With eight engines racing, just watch them fly!
A team full of elves printed presents all year
On the planet North Pole with the magic reindeer.
Space Santa! Watch him fly
Space Santa! He's our guy
Space Santa! Bringing gifts to all
Space Santa! Space Santa!

Someone shoves a beaker into my hand. It looks like eggnog, but the fumes indicate a high level of alcohol. I hand it off to someone else as I make my way through the crowd. Puffs of white cottony "snow" lie in drifts at the base of the float tubes. A stray tuft wafts up inside the tube as I watch. Shaking my head, I step into the tube and follow.

At Level 20, the party continues. Here the decorations are blue and white instead of red and green, and a two-meter-tall dreidel spins above our heads. Someone shoves a glass of blue liquid at me, shouting *"Martzel Pop!"*

I battle my way through the horde, throwing a few gentle hip-checks along the way. Ducking into Radial 7, I hurry out-station and turn again at

C Ring. The sounds of the party fade to a muted rumble, and I wave my ring at an access door.

Ducking through the entry, I scramble through the quiet bot duct, bent almost double to avoid the pipes above my head. Some of the bot access ducts are tall enough to allow easy access for workers, but in these older, lower levels, a lot of them have been modified over time. The conduits have been added for additional wiring and plumbing. The space above them is often illegally co-opted by residents, providing extra storage. Sometimes it's rented out on the black market to bring in extra credits.

A few meters in, I reach bot 23D. It's humming quietly, so I tap the control panel. The tiny screen lights up and shows all systems green. "Why are you just sitting here?" I ask, but the bot doesn't answer. Which is a good thing—they don't have voice response.

I run diagnostics, just to confirm the green screen, but nothing pops up. Crawling over the bot, I check underneath and all around. Nothing on the floor that would stop it from moving. Some of the bots are designed to follow painted cues on the floor, but this is not one of those bots. And the floor is clean. I hit the resume button, then jump away as the bot tries to continue on its pre-programmed route. It stops harmlessly a couple centimeters from my legs. Looking up, I spot the girders from which the conduits are suspended. I grab the girder and pull my legs up, in the kind of crunch I've seen Kara do. As soon as my legs are out of the way, the bot putters beneath me and away on its business.

I drop back onto my feet. Fixing bots and getting a workout at the same time—way to multitask Triana! I rub my stomach, wondering if one crunch counts as working out. It's Christmas, so yeah, it does.

The bot bleeps again, stopping about ten meters away. Maybe there's a loose chip or wire. This is going to take some major diagnostic work. Opening the command screen via my holo-ring, I flick the "suspend the route" button and input a "return to garage" command. Execute another perfect gymnastic feat to allow the bot to head back the way we both came. Two crunches—maybe I'll reward myself with one of those sticky pastries when I get back to Level 2.

With a yelp, I swing up into a third crunch as the repair drone I sent up earlier whizzes toward me, hot on the trail of the vacu-bot. I am definitely getting the sticky bun.

I wander further up the duct. Obviously, the repair drone never reached the stalled bot. Maybe there was something up here causing the trouble. I reach a cross duct. A movement to my right draws my eyes. Then I do a double take.

A young-looking man with flowing white-blond hair sits cross-legged in the center of the duct. His head is bowed, his powerful shoulders nearly touch the duct sides, and a snug red shirt stretches across his abs and pecs.

I straighten in surprise and bang my head against the conduit. "Fork!"

The man's head pops up, and his startling blue eyes fix on me. "Spoon?" he replies uncertainly.

Rubbing my head, I step closer. "Who are you? And what are you doing in my bot duct?"

He cocks his head, as if considering my question. "Is this your duct?"

"I'm a maintenance tech, so yeah, it's my duct," I say, belligerent. "Who are you?"

He shakes his head, his thick hair swinging around his face. "I don't have a good answer for you."

"Look, if you're too drunk to remember your name, I can get you some BuzzKill and send you on your way." I've encountered lost partiers before. "I won't call security. But you can't stay here."

He pushes a hand through his hair. "I don't feel drunk. I just don't remember my name." His eyes widen. "Or how I got here. Or where I came from."

"What do you remember?" I ran into some criminals a few months ago who used a memory-wiping drug. Maybe this guy got a dose somehow.

The guy's stomach growls, loudly. "I definitely don't remember when I ate last." He smiles at me, the expression lighting up his face. "Would you like to join me for dinner?"

TWO

I GIVE the guy a flat look. "If that's a pickup line, it needs work. Besides, I have a boyfriend." Kind of. He's gone a lot, and frankly, I'm never quite sure what our status is. "Anyway, it's closer to lunchtime."

He shakes his head, his blond hair swishing. "Not a line. I really am hungry, and I'd prefer not to eat alone." He reaches into his pocket, pulls out a pile of paper and coins, and laughs. It's a deep, sexy laugh. "It seems I have some cash, so my treat."

Looking at the wad in his hand, my eyes widen. "You've got a lot of credits there. You might want to put those away before we head out into the station. Level 20 is not a great place to be flashing cash around, unless you're *Sprzężaj*." At his blank look, I elaborate. "Poelish Mafia? They run the mid-levels of the station."

"So, we're on a space station?" he asks conversationally as I lead the way toward the duct exit.

My head whips around, and I bonk it on the overhead again. "Fork!" I rub my head. "You didn't even know you're on the station?"

He shrugs, his bent over position making the movement awkward. We half-crawl, half-walk the rest of the way out of the duct in silence.

Finally exiting the duct, the man stands up. Fully upright and in the good light of the C Ring, the guy is even better looking. The icy blond hair frames high cheekbones, a straight nose, and those sapphire blue eyes. The red fabric of his shirt stretches across powerful pecs, strong biceps, and tight abs. His jeans are snug enough to show off solid thighs, but not too tight, leaving some things to the imagination. My temperature ratchets up a few degrees, and I feel like fanning myself like those ladies in the ancient history vids.

I drag my eyes upward and find him grinning at me. My face flushes, but luckily my caramel skin doesn't show the blush too badly. "Come on," I say, grumpily. "I'll take you to my favorite noodle place. You're buying."

WE FACE each other across a red plas tablecloth with the words Hot-Good Noodles splashed in white. We plug our orders into the wait-bot and send it on its way. "So, what should I call you?" I fiddle with a chopstick.

He gives me that considering look again and shrugs. "Dunno. What do I look like? A Dave?" His eyes twinkle. "A Rudolpho?" He flutters his eyelashes. "How about Doctor Intense?" He lowers his brows and stares at me through narrowed eyes.

"I'm going to call you Fabio."

"Because I'm fabulous?"

"Because you look like a guy from the *Ancient TēVē* vids who was named Fabio." I poke the chopstick at him. "Practically a dead ringer."

He mutters the name to himself a couple times. "Nope, not feeling it. How about Scott?"

"Why Scott? That doesn't sound as fabulous." The wait-bot trundles up and opens its cargo door to reveal steaming bowls. I pull them out and put one in front of each of us.

He shrugs. "Just sounds like a good name. Someone trustworthy and helpful. A friend."

"Scott it is, then," I scoop up some noodles. "I'm Triana, by the way."

We eat in silence except for the slurping of noodles. Scott polishes off the first bowl in record time and orders a second. "That was delicious. I feel like I haven't eaten in weeks. Do they have cake here?"

"We can find some cake later." Or one of those sticky buns. "Right now, we need to talk about you. Who are you? What are you doing here? Do you have a holo-ring?"

"What's a holo-ring?" He eagerly pulls his second bowl from the bot.

"You're kidding, right? Everyone has a holo-ring." I flick my ring and a browser pops up in palm. "It's how we connect to the net." I flick through a few screens and a vid of Fabio pops up. "I guess you don't look as much like him as I thought." The fact is Fabio looks like Scott's less attractive, older brother.

"That's pretty neat," Scott says. "Can I get one?"

"Can we focus?"

Scott shrugs and goes back to his bowl. "What are we focusing on?"

I sigh. "Who you are? If you don't have a holo-ring, you aren't from the station. You must be from one of the ships. Let's find you a place to stay, and I'll see what I can find out."

My ring pings, and a message pops up. Bot 23D has returned to the garage; no problem reports. "Zark!" I jump up out of my chair. "I'm supposed to be working! I gotta get back to the MCC." Somehow, the need to help Scott completely overrode my common sense. It's like I totally forgot I was in the middle of a workday.

Scott picks up his bowl and slurps down the last of the noodles. He wipes his mouth and smiles. "I'm ready when you are."

"Come on. I need to hand you off to security and get back to work. You can't come to the MCC with me."

Scott nods. "Okay. Whatever you think is best."

We take the float tubes up to Level 40, and I direct him to the door of the security office. "These guys can run a DNA check and figure out where you belong. Thanks for lunch, but I gotta run. Give me a call when you get it all figured out."

"How would I do that?" he asks.

"Oh, you don't have a holo." I think for a moment. "Just ask them to send me a message. Triana Moore, in Maintenance. They can get it to me."

He nods as the door slides open. "Thanks for your help, Triana Moore of Maintenance."

I smile. "You're welcome, Scott of the bot duct."

BACK IN THE MCC, I'm surprised to see no maintenance calls in the queue. Nothing went wrong while I was gone. The bots all performed perfectly. Maybe I should play hooky more often.

I pull up vids from the bot duct where I found Scott. I give myself a mental head slap. I was so distracted by him, I forgot to check the cams while I was out there! But the "cam down" banner is gone. Checking the vids, it appears the cams came back online as soon as Scott and I exited the duct. In fact, the first frames are a glimpse of me closing the duct access door behind us.

I switch to the cams outside in C Ring, but they went down seconds before the duct cams came back up. Incredulous, I pull up a series of temporary cam outages that follow our progress through the station. This can't be real.

- Level 20 concourse: cams down for ninety seconds at exactly the time we took the float tube up to Level 23.
- Level 23 concourse: cams down for sixty-five seconds while we crossed to the noodle place.
- Hot-Good Noodles: cams out for twenty-seven minutes at exactly the time we were there.
- Level 23 concourse: down again for fifty-three seconds.
- Level 40 concourse: down for forty-eight seconds.
- Radial 6 cams: down for eighty-three seconds.

I pull up the security office, but their internal cams are working fine. Except there's no footage of Scott. Scrolling back and forth more frantically now, I can't find any visual evidence of him. The cams outside the security office were dead. They came back on as I left the area—just after Scott went through the door. But the vid inside the office never wavered. At the time Scott should have gone in, the vid shows the door sliding open and closed.

No one walked in.

I rub my face. I didn't drink any of the libations flowing so freely out in the concourse. We didn't stop at the WackyWeed Bakery. What is going on? How could Scott be disrupting cams? How did he not show up inside the security office?

THREE

The Shuttle Dock on Level 4 is my favorite bar, although tonight, it's louder than usual. Something about the holiday spirit, I guess. I tap in an order, and the bar bot brings me a beer. My roommate Kara and her boyfriend Erco are supposed to meet me for a drink. Erco came up from the planet today, to spend Christmas with Kara. Since Ty, my sort-of boyfriend, is on a mission dirt-side, I didn't bother going back to our compartment to change. My station coveralls blend in nicely at the Shuttle Dock.

"Hey Moore, how's bots?" Farquad, who works in Ops, hollers as he strolls by with a guy wearing pink scrubs. I wave and smile as they continue on. A couple guards from the detention cells on Level 1 eye the empty stools at my table hopefully, but I shake my head and they walk away.

"Is this seat taken?" a deep voice asks.

I look up, and there's Scott. He's so beautiful he takes my breath away for an instant. I shake my head. "I have friends coming. If you can find another chair, you can join us." That challenge should take several minutes on this crowded night. Maybe I can get my thoughts together.

He returns almost immediately with another tall chair and squeezes it in beside me.

"How did you find a stool so fast?" I demand.

He gives me that million-watt smile. "People like to help me."

"Yeah, like the people in the Security office?" I give him the stink eye. "How did you do that?"

He blinks those beautiful blue eyes. "Do what?"

"Any of it! Disrupt my bots? Interrupt the cams? Not go into the security office? I checked the security logs—you never arrived there, even after I watched you walk through the door."

"How'd you check the security logs?" he counters. "Never mind. Can you show me how to order a beer?"

I stab at the table and point to the list of beers on the auto bar menu. "Take your pick. As to how did I check the logs? I'm a maint tech. I have access to everything on this station." Not officially, but I have no problems accessing data. I've been known to hack a bit.

Scott selects a beer and feeds some bills into the table slot I indicate. "I didn't want to bother the security folks. I figured you could help me just as well, without leaving any official record. It occurred to me that I could get in trouble for being here without proper ID or authorizations or something."

A tray descends from the ceiling, holding a frosty mug. Scott takes the beer, and the robotic arm snaps the tray vertical, then ascends and scoots back through the opening in the wall. "Fancy."

"Bar bots are faster, cheaper, and more reliable than human waiters." I gesture up to the bar boss on the catwalk above the room. "She's keeping an eye on the whole place and can fix the bot arms if they malfunction. They use hover delivery in the upper levels, but the lower levels are the older parts of the station. If the old tech ain't broke, we don't fix it."

We watch in silence for a few minutes as robotic arms deliver drinks and snacks all around the room. A holo pops up on my table and asks if I'd like another beverage. I wave my holo-ring through the "yes, same order" icon, authorizing payment. I pick up the glass and drain the last centimeter as the robot arm delivers another. This time, the tray stays horizontal, allowing me to return my glass.

"The sales prompt is triggered by the level of liquid in your glass, so if you don't want any more, leave a couple gulps in the bottom. Otherwise, you'll have to keep fending off the ads." I fix my eyes on him. "But don't think you can distract me with your vid actor looks and your helpless tourist attitude. I want to know what you're doing to my cams."

A thought hits me, and I flick my holo-ring. As I suspected, the OS vid feeds from the Shuttle Dock Bar are offline. I stab my finger at the holo. "How are you doing that?"

Scott shakes his head. "I'm not doing anything. What are you even showing me?"

"Everywhere you go, the cams stop working. You're completely invisible to the station OS." I probably shouldn't have told him that.

"I can see why that would bother you." He takes a long drink from his mug. "You all like to keep an eye on things. Very big brother of you."

I give him a puzzled look but ignore his statement. "How are you doing it?"

"I don't know. I'm not doing it on purpose. Maybe it's my magnetic personality." He grins, eyes twinkling.

I punch down the warmth in my stomach. "Stop using your Fabio charm on me. I want to know what's going on."

He holds up his hands. "I really don't know. Maybe if I remembered who I am, it would all make sense, but right now, I haven't a clue."

I grind my teeth. "That's what security was supposed to help with, remember? DNA check?"

"You have access to everything." He blinks those huge, blue eyes innocently at me. "Can't you do the check? Off the record?"

I growl, but he's saved when Kara and Erco pick that exact moment to arrive.

"Who's the hottie?" Kara whispers as Erco and Scott bump fists. "If I wasn't taken, I'd be all over that." She eyes him up and down, admiring his tight black jeans, the thin forest green sweater clinging to his chest, and his flowing blond hair.

"Hey." I point a finger at Scott. "Where'd you get those clothes?"

He grins, shoving the sleeves up over his strong, lightly haired forearms. A tattoo encircles his left wrist and spirals up into his sleeve. It looks like some kind of vine. "There's a sale up on 37. I got a locker at the spaceport and went shopping. Good thing I have some money." He turns to Kara and

Erco. "I seem to have some amnesia, and Triana here is going to help me find my way home."

Erco and Kara exclaim; Scott gives them the rundown. I watch him through narrowed eyes. Who is he, and what is he really trying to pull? He has a charisma that is mesmerizing. When he speaks, it becomes difficult to focus on anything else. As he wraps up his story, Kara drags her eyes away from him.

"What does Ty think about all this?" she asks me.

"Who's Ty?" Scott lifts an eyebrow.

"Ty O'Neill, board security agent." Erco waves at me. "He and Triana are kind of a thing. Super good guy. He can help you, I'm sure."

I roll my eyes. "I'm perfectly capable of helping Scott myself. Besides, O'Neill isn't even on-station right now. No—" I cut Kara off. "I haven't talked to him today. No reason to bother him about this."

Kara smiles. "Good move. You wouldn't want him all hot and bothered by," she pauses, lazily looking Scott up and down, "all this."

Scott winks at Kara.

Ugh. "I'm not hiding anything. We'll be talking tonight." But hopefully I'll have Scott sorted out before then.

My holo buzzes, interrupting with a priority one call. The voice in my audio implant sets my teeth on edge. "Would you excuse me a moment," I say to the table in general. "The Ice Dame calls."

I send the call to hold and stride out of the bar. Around the corner and down the radial there's a little alcove that provides some privacy. Unfortunately, it's currently occupied. I tap the closest shoulder. Pointing to the maint tech patch on my shoulder, I say, "Atmo leak," and the two scramble away. Idiot civilians. How could there be an atmosphere leak this far *inside* the station?

Leaning against the wall, I put the call through. "Sorry to keep you waiting, Mother." I'm not.

"Annabelle, I require assistance." Is that an edge of panic in the Ice Dame's voice? Unheard of.

"You need my help? Where's Hy-Mi?" Hy-Mi is mother's personal assistant and has been organizing the little details of her life for longer than

I've been around. Mother runs SK2, and Hy-Mi keeps her under control—which keeps the rest of us from leaping out an airlock.

"Hy-Mi is handling the party. I need help with something else. Come up. I'll expect you in ten minutes." I wish I could ignore the summons, but since Dame Morgan authorizes the paychecks—I know when to shut up and color.

"Gotta go help the Ice Dame," I tell Kara, Erco, and Scott when I get back to the table. "Some Christmas party disaster, I'm sure." I give Kara a hug and whisper, "I'll stay upstairs tonight."

Scott follows me out the door.

I stop and face him. "Where are you going?"

"I'm coming to help you. I'm excellent at Christmas party disasters."

I narrow my eyes. "Really? You don't know your name, but you know you're good at party disasters."

He shakes his head. "I know I'm good at *Christmas*. I don't know how I know, but I do."

"Ok," I say, eyeing him speculatively. "But security is going to run a DNA search at the door."

"Excellent! Two birds with one stone." He smiles and gestures to the concourse.

We take the float tubes up to Level 82. Am I crazy to take this guy up to the penthouse? I know nothing about him, except that he disrupts cams. Talk about a perfect opportunity for a terrorist! But somehow, I trust Scott, even when all my common sense is trying to convince me otherwise.

I open the old-fashioned door next to the float tube. Scott follows me through, into a small, well-appointed lobby.

"Good evening Sera Morgan." The guard sitting behind the high counter slides off his chair and to his feet.

"Hey, Rafe. Can you do a visitor pass for Scott, here?" I gesture to my companion.

Scott puts his hand on the scan plate, and winces when the tiny needle bites his finger. We wait as the system chugs through its data. Finally, a tiny square pops out of a slot on the desk. Scott and I lean forward to look.

"The system says you don't use a holo-ring," Rafe says in surprise. He picks up the pass, a clear patch about a centimeter square. "Please hold out your left hand, Ser Calvin." Rafe smooths the patch onto the back of Scott's hand, where it disappears. "This is an accompanied pass. Please stay with an authorized resident of the level at all times."

Scott grins. "I'll stick to her like glue."

"Hey Rafe, can I see your screen?" I ask.

"Sure," he replies but then he swears. "Sorry Sera Morgan, but the data went blank." He taps a few icons. "I can't get it back!"

"What did it say about Scott, I mean, Ser Calvin?" I ask.

He shrugs. "It had a green banner, so I didn't read the details. It said he was authorized guest access and didn't have a holo. I'm sure you can look him up." He gives me a perplexed look.

"Of course I can. No big deal." I gesture to the float tube behind Rafe's desk. "After you, Ser Calvin."

At the top of the float tube, we step out into another lobby. This larger room contains plush seating groups, live flower arrangements, and a grand piano. An attractive woman dressed in green and red velvet with white trim is playing Christmas standards, even though no one is in the room. I always wonder if Rafe lets her know when someone is coming, and she just starts mid-song.

"Good evening Sera Morgan, Ser Calvin," she says. Question answered— she definitely got a heads-up from downstairs.

Scott smiles broadly. "Merry Christmas, dear lady."

With a roll of my eyes, I grab him by the arm and steer him towards the door marked A. "Scott Calvin," I say. Why does that name sound familiar? I shake my head. "Does that ring any bells?"

"Not really. Why are they calling you Sera Morgan? I thought your name was Moore."

I puff out a breath and my hair bounces. "My birth name is Annabelle Morgan. I ran away when I was eighteen and became a 'space janitor,' as my mother likes to call me. It's a long story."

He shrugs. "I've got nowhere to go. Literally."

I wave my holo-ring at compartment A, and the door slides open, silent and efficient. As we step into the foyer, it closes behind us, cutting off the strains of *Christmas in Andromeda.*

The compartment looks like someone hired home decor elves who drank too much coffee and had an unlimited budget at Kacey's Kristmas Kastle. Fragrant Kakuvian pine boughs cascade down the curving staircase. A huge tree stands by the windows, covered in twinkling silver lights, sparkling silver ornaments, and glittering silver tinsel. Every vase, frame, and knickknack in the place shines in green and silver glory.

Even the furniture has been reupholstered in shades of dark green and silver. In the center of the room, a woman wearing red velvet droops despondently on the edge of a green velvet armchair.

"Beautiful!" Scott says. "The room, the tree, that dress! So festive!"

I stare at him. "Dial it back, brown-noser," I mutter. Turning to the woman, I wave toward Scott. "Mother, may I present Scott Calvin? Scott, this is Dame Imogen Morgan."

Mother raises her head. She's well over sixty, but rejuvenation treatments and expensive aesthetics make her look more like my sister than my mother. My younger sister, if I'm honest with myself. Her honey blonde hair spills down her back, almost to her waist. Ice-blue eyes, perfectly shaped brows, and high cheekbones give her oval face the look of a storybook princess.

She smiles sadly at Scott. "Delighted to meet you, Ser Calvin, but I wasn't expecting any guests. Just my daughter."

"Annabelle said you had a Christmas emergency," Scott says, "and that's my specialty. How can I be of service?"

Mother rises so gracefully she seems to levitate off the chair. They tried to teach me to move like that when I was younger, but I just never got the hang of it. "It's nothing, Ser. Just a minor family issue."

He laughs his deep, rich chuckle. "Call me Scott. And is there really any such thing as a 'minor' family issue? Please, let me help."

Maybe I can leave Scott to help and go back to the Shuttle Dock. What woman wouldn't be happy with a handsome guy like him to do her bidding?

Mother reaches a limp hand to me. "Annabelle, dear, thank you for coming to help me."

I roll my eyes. "Scott, would you excuse us for a moment?" I offer him a seat, call a bev-bot to take his drink order, and chivvy my mother into the office.

Shutting the door, I turn around and stare at the Ice Dame. "Cut the crap, Mother. This depressed damsel in distress thing is really not a good look for you."

My mother fixes her icy blue eyes on me. "Just come up on your own, next time," she snaps. "I have a reputation to maintain."

I laugh. "Everyone knows you're a shrewd and ruthless businesswoman. I'm not sure what game you're playing."

She points a finger at the door. "You brought him into this house. I'm trying to salvage the situation."

"You know who he is?" I'm about to ask but realize I can't admit I brought a total stranger into the most secure part of the station. "Do you want me to take him away?"

"Of course, I don't want you to take him away! Treat him with respect! We can't have him thinking we're anything but the most civilized of families."

Now I'm really wondering who this guy is. Who could put the legendary Ice Dame into such a tizzy? "What did you want help with, Mother?"

"We can talk later. We've kept him waiting too long." She opens the door. "So sorry to leave you alone, Ser Cal— Scott."

Mother fawns all over Scott for a full forty-five minutes. I listen closely, but don't get any additional clues to his identity. Sitting back in the couch, I sigh heavily.

Mistake. Mother turns those icy eyes on me. "Did you need something, dear?" Her voice drips menace.

"I was just wondering if Dav left anything tasty in the kitchen. Would you like some dessert, Scott?" I smile at Mother. Let's see her get out of that.

She doesn't. "Excellent idea, dear. Why don't you go see what you can scare up?"

Scott tries to demur, but I'm off the couch like a rocket, and out the door before he can open his mouth. He wanted to come up here—he can deal with the Ice Dame.

In the kitchen, I find some mini Kinturky Bourbon Beacan Tarts. Sliding them onto a plate, I start the coffee maker and pull up my link to the OS. I run searches on Scott Calvin, pull up lists of important CEOs, and even try searching on "reclusive non-holo-using powerbroker." Nothing comes up. I start a facial recognition program I borrowed from my former friend Glitch. It will take a while, but it's the best.

Taking a deep breath, I grab the tray and head back into the living room.

"You're amazing!" Mother coos. A chill crawls across my shoulders at the tone of her voice—so out of character for her. "That's the perfect idea! Annabelle, dear, Scott has come up with the perfect gift for R'ger. You're off the hook."

I set the tray down on the coffee table and stare at her. "That was your big emergency? You needed a present for R'ger?"

Picking up her coffee cup, she turns her gaze on me. "Showing our loved ones that we care for them is what Christmas is all about. But I'm sure you have had the perfect gift for Agent O'Neill for months." She smiles, a viciously delighted smile.

Zark! I haven't gotten anything for O'Neill.

FOUR

I put my plate down on the tray, and gulp down the last of my coffee. "Scott and I should be going, Mother. Scott needs to check in at the hotel, and I promised to show him down."

"Nonsense," the Ice Dame replies. "Ser Calvin can't stay in a hotel. I have a perfectly good guest suite going empty. You'll stay here with me, won't you, Scott?"

Zark.

"He has a reservation—" I start to say, but Scott interrupts.

"I really don't want to impose." He puts his fork on his plate. "That was the best Beacan Tart I've had in ages. Your pastry chef is amazing."

"Yes, Dav is a treasure. The Gates have been trying to steal him for years." Mother smiles complacently. "If you stay, you can try his waffles in the morning. They are to die for."

I can't believe that phrase came out of her mouth. She's really channeling her inner fangirl.

Scott shrugs and looks at me, his blue eyes sparkling. "You've convinced me. I can't say no to Dav's waffles!"

I stomp up the stairs behind Scott and my gushing mother. She points out the famous paintings and sculptures as we climb, describing the special security built into the external walls of the station. She gestures toward the hallway to the private suites, stopping just short of winking at Scott as she does. I try not to vomit and think about bringing up R'ger's name.

"Annabelle's room is the first on the left," she tells Scott.

I gasp—is she trying to pimp me out?

"This is the guest suite." Mother waves the door open. "Annabelle will send a code to your ID patch, so you can access it." She doesn't even glance my direction, as if I'm some menial employee. Well, I guess I am, but I'm also her daughter. Although to be fair, I usually don't want her to remember that. "I'll leave you here. Enjoy your night." She actually winks at Scott this time then disappears down the hall.

I grind my teeth and shove Scott into the guest suite. He opens his mouth, but I fling up a hand. Scrolling through the OS, I double check that Scott's disruptor effect is still working. "Okay, who the heck *are* you?" I growl as soon as I'm sure she can't eavesdrop.

Scott grins at me. "I guess I must be someone pretty important. I can't remember ever being the object of that much brown-nosing. Of course, I can't remember anything before this morning, so there's that."

"Seriously, cut the crap." I spit the words out. "The system recognized and tagged you as a VIP. What kind of scam are you running?"

I drop onto the love seat. Like all the guest suites on the penthouse level, it's plush. Thick carpet conceals the deck and luxurious fabrics cover the walls and the plush modern furniture. Like all bedrooms up here, it's an internal room. Protection from stray meteors while they slept won out over dramatic views for the top-levs. There's a spacelight—a window in the ceiling that allows occupants to see the stars—but it isn't real. The scene is projected by expensive equipment to provide a life-like experience. There are actually several meters of titanium overhead.

The large room holds a small seating area with loveseat and reclining massage chair, a large bookcase that blocks part of the room, and a huge bed hidden behind that. A full bath opens off the far end of the room, beyond the bed. A small AutoKich'n is hidden inside built-in cabinets made of real Kakuvian Oak—thick, heavy wood that screams privilege on a space station made of materials that had to be launched into orbit.

Scott sits down beside me, and I flick open the OS. I pull up the security system, worming my way into the restricted databases. The file Rafe saw has to be stored in here somewhere.

"Don't forget to give me access to the door," Scott says.

"I'm not giving you access to anything until I know who you are," I mutter. "At least this way I know you can't sneak out and murder us in our sleep."

Scott's face falls. "I would never harm anyone! How can you suggest such a thing?"

"If you really have no idea who you are, you don't know that's true, do you?" I snap. "And if you're lying about your memory loss, I have a very good reason to not trust you. Besides, it's not like I'm locking you up in a cell with a metal toilet. You could live happily in here for months."

Scott looks around the room and nods thoughtfully. "I guess you're right."

"Zark! This file has nothing!" I flip through the screens. "Here's the approval. It says 'cleared for VIP guest access' and your name. But nothing else! How did the system even identify you as this Ser Calvin? Wait a minute." I flick a couple more details then narrow my eyes at him. "This says you're Scott Calvin. If your memory is so faulty, how'd you manage to pick your actual, *real* first name?"

Scott holds up his hands. "I don't know. Maybe it's buried deep in my brain and managed to surface. I told you it felt right. Better than 'Fabio'!" He bumps his shoulder into mine.

I conquer the desire to smile back at him. "Something's not right. I am definitely not giving you access to the door. You'll stay here for the night, where I can make sure you're not causing any havoc."

I stomp out of the room before I can change my mind, making sure it shuts and locks behind me. As I walk to my own room, I set up motion-activated cam alerts outside his door, and double check the latches. I want to know if he manages to get out.

FIVE

Back in my childhood bedroom, I lay on the bed and stare blankly at the space-light. How could I have forgotten to get a Christmas present for O'Neill? My brain spins as I try to come up with a suitable gift. What do you get for the guy who might be your boyfriend? A tiny voice in my head suggests I ask Scott, but I squash it back down.

A vibration from my holo-ring wakes me from a light doze. The facial recognition app has found a match! I flick the icon and pull up the file.

Match: Scott Calvin.

THAT'S ALL IT SAYS.

No catalog of pictures and videos from cams around the station. No information about planet of origin, occupation, education, nothing. No financial links. None of the information this app normally presents. Just to test, I take a selfie and run it through the system. Within minutes, it pulls up both my names, my certification from the Techno-Inst, my current occupation, my station clearances, random pics and vid of me in the public parts of the station, everything.

I pull pics of friends and family from my personal files and run them through the system. R'ger takes the longest, since he's the oldest, yet newest to the station, but eventually it pulls even his date and location of birth. Zark, he's OLD!

I drum my fingers on the bedspread, totally flummoxed. How can the system identify Scott's name but nothing else?

A call on my holo wakes me again. I smile—it's Ty.

"Hey," I say, brilliantly.

"Hey, yourself." He gives me that smile that sends a heat-wave through my chest. "Sorry to call so late, but I figured on a Friday night you'd be asleep on the sofa after watching *Ancient Tēvē*."

"Close, but no." I flip the holo up onto the ceiling and lay back on the bed, looking up at him. "I'm up on 83, laying on my bed, *not* watching *Ancient Tēvē*."

Ty stares. "Really? Of your own volition? Blink twice if I need to come break you out."

"Like she could keep me here." I laugh, then sober. "No, there's some weird stuff going on." I give him the run-down on Scott Calvin.

"So, you didn't have a clue who he was, but let Rafe pass him through to 83?" Ty's voice sounds strangled. "You know you're going to give me a heart attack."

"Better check if they have a defibrillator down there. But I figured Rafe must know who he was. In fact, I let him come up because I figured the board sec system would identify him." I rub my eyes. "Does it do this often?"

"Allow unknown interlopers access to the chair of the board? No." His face is hard. Zark, he's mad at me.

"No, I mean identify someone as a VIP but completely hide the data used to make that decision." I hope so.

"You wish." But he looks thoughtful. "Although, there are certain individuals who might trigger that kind of secure approval, at least at the guard station. But you have access to everything I do—you should be able to see his details."

"Maybe it's above your pay grade," I joke.

He gives me a look. "Maybe. Look, I just want to know you're safe. Then I won't worry."

"I've got motion detectors set outside his room," I reassure him. "And if his magic cam-scrambling effect turns off those detectors, the scrambling itself will activate an alarm." I pull up the cam files. "He hasn't moved from his room. Unless he can sneak out through the spacelight." I laugh.

"Not even undocumented VIPs can do that." He settles back into his chair. "Still, you could go stay at my place."

"And leave Mother up here alone with him? I brought him up—he's my responsibility." I grin fiendishly. "More importantly, I want to get in on Dav's waffles in the morning."

"Ah ha! I knew there was a real reason."

We chat a few more minutes, but he starts yawning. "Why don't you go to bed? I'll talk to you tomorrow."

THE WAFFLES EXCEED EXPECTATIONS, as always. And, yes, I know that's implausible, but so are Dav's waffles. Light and fluffy, sweet or savory, topped with fruit, syrups, whipped cream, fried eggs, sautéed vegetables, anything you can imagine. Dav's food never disappoints.

"Please, Ser Calvin— Scott. Stay and enjoy for as long as you like." Mother pats her lips with a linen napkin and rises. "Unfortunately, I have meetings to attend, so I must depart. Annabelle, please bring Ser Calvin by my office before you leave." She sails out of the room.

As soon as she's safely behind closed doors, Dav emerges from the kitchen. "That woman is driving me crazy!" he hisses.

I stare at Dav in surprise. He never refers to his employer in that tone. "Is she demanding miniature ice sculptures again?"

When I was a kid, she insisted on having a tiny carved ice sculpture at each place setting. Of course, mini-ice sculptures become puddles about twenty minutes after you put them out, but Mother insisted. Dav's final solution involved a specially built table with tiny temperature fields by each plate. The table cost a fortune and was never used again.

Dav blinks at me. "No, no, of course not. I wish. We still have that stupid table in storage. No, I was talking about her." He jerks a thumb over his shoulder.

"Who? Did you hire an assistant? Heaven knows you could use one for the holiday season." I peer beyond him, but the door to the kitchen is closed.

Scott leans back in his seat and watches us silently.

"She's an intern," Dav growls. "She's done a half year at the Culinary Institute of Kaku, and she's here between terms. She thinks she knows everything."

"Why don't you fire her?" I ask.

"She's Don Huatang's granddaughter," Dav whispers.

I groan. "*Gloria* is interning in your kitchen? She didn't attend the Culinary Institute! She's been here on station all year."

"It's a virtual program, specifically developed for top-lev students who can't commit to a long period in one location." Dav pinches the bridge of his nose.

Scott sits up. "Virtual culinary school? That's a thing?"

"It's a thing for top-levs who will never work in the field and just want to accrue degrees. Most of them never get through the first year because it requires too much effort." My lip curls. That very program was one of the reasons I ran away and changed my name. I wanted a real degree, not a gold-leaf embossed virtual sheepskin.

"Talk to Mother," I tell Dav. "She'd love a reason to stick it to Don Huatang's family. I can't believe she even allowed Gloria in her home."

Dav drops his head into his hands. "I didn't tell her it was Gloria. An old friend from the CIK begged me to take her on, and I was afraid Dame Morgan would say no. So, I just asked her if I could bring in an intern. I didn't mention who it was. And Dame Morgan didn't care, as long as she passed the security checks, which, of course Gloria didn't even need. I didn't realize how awful she would be!"

A crash and a screech ring out from the kitchen. Dav leaps to his feet. "Oh Holy Night, what is she doing now? I have two hundred figgy puddings steaming in there!" He lunges to the kitchen door.

Before he reaches it, the door slides open. Gloria appears, steam billowing out around her. She's wearing traditional chef's garb of black and white checked pants and a pristine white coat with a tiny red CIK logo on the shoulder. The jacket has been altered to fit tight to her torso, with a very low-cut, scoop neckline to show off her enormous boobs. "Oh, Chef, you might want to check your equipment. It appears to be malfunctioning."

With a growl, Dav pushes past her out of the room, while Gloria saunters toward us. She smiles at me, her hair a wild, red halo around her head. "I thought this look was appropriate for the help." She says, gently tugging a strand.

I grit my teeth, resisting the urge to push my own naturally red curls out of my eyes. "Don't you have some dishes to wash, Gloria?"

She ignores me, transferring her attention to Scott. "Good morning, sexy! If I'd known you were here, I would have volunteered to serve breakfast." She practically purrs as she sashays to him, hips swaying. She leans over his shoulder, reaching forward to pick up the coffee pot. Her ample bosom rubs against his arm.

"Cream, two sugars," Scott says, not looking at her. "And I'd like another bagel, thanks." Without missing a beat, he smiles at me. "What are we doing today, Annabelle?"

Gloria's teeth grind and she snaps upright. "Get your own coffee." She stomps away.

"That was awesome," I say as the kitchen door closes behind her. "If you can think of a way to get rid of her completely, I'm sure Dav would supply you with waffles for a lifetime. She's probably in there sabotaging his entire menu."

Scott shrugs. "It should be easy enough to engineer a catastrophic spill. There's a reason chefs normally wear long sleeves and high necked jackets. Why doesn't he do that?"

I shake my head. "Dav would never purposely sacrifice food. Think of something else."

"I'll work on it." He pushes back his chair and stands, then holds out a hand to me. "Shall we escape this gilded cage?"

We say our farewells to Mother, after assuring her we will return that night for the Christmas party. I really don't want to come, but Scott eagerly accepts, so I agree.

"You're going to regret that," I mutter as we step out into the Level 83 lobby. "SK'Corp parties are SO boring. Lots of corporate stooges kissing up to board members. It wouldn't be too bad if you could drink enough to take the edge off, but Mother spikes the food with BuzzKill. Only Nicolai Bezos manages to drink enough to stay tipsy." We cross to the float tubes.

"Hey, Ammabelle!" A slurred voice warbles. "You lookin' for me?"

I spin around. Nicolai Bezos sprawls across one of the heavy couches, waving a mug at me.

"Speak of the devil."

Nicolai sits up and holds out a flask. "Egg mog! You wan' some?"

"Nick, it's nine in the morning." I take a few steps toward him. "Have you been drinking all night?" As I approach, a waft of alcohol, stale sweat, and a twinge of vomit assault my nose. Nick's bloodshot eyes peer at me from between puffy lids. His clothes are wrinkled, stained, and stiff.

He shrugs. "All might, all day, whatever. It'sh Chrishmash! I love egg mog. Hoosh yer frien'?"

"That's Scott. I don't think he wants any eggnog, either. You should go home, Nick."

Scott steps over and reaches out a hand. Nicolai bumps fists. With a twist of his wrist, Scott grips Nick's hand and pops him up off the couch. Scott swings him around and gets a shoulder under his arm. "Let's get you home, friend."

I direct Scott to the Bezos' door. Fortunately, Dame Bezos's personal assistant responds to the doorbell. She takes one look at Nick and turns to us. "Thanks for bringing him home, Sera Morgan. He's been drinking more and more since Bobby Putin left."

I grimace and pass Nick off to her. "Can you handle him by yourself?"

"I'm fine." Nick straightens up. "I just need to get some sleep. Long night, too much booze."

We stare at him. His face is a little green, but his voice is unslurred and he's steady on his feet. I look at Scott. "Did you slip him some Buzzkill?"

Scott shakes his head. "Nope, don't have any of that on me. Besides, I think it would have taken a whole bottle to sober him up."

"Annabelle, Scott, thanks for bringing me home." Nicolai nods to each of us in turn. "But I have a splitting headache. Keandra, would you get me a med pack?" He disappears into the compartment.

We all shrug at each other and Keandra closes the door. Scott and I walk across the lobby.

I pause by the float tube. "That was weird."

"Who's Bobby?" Scott asks. "His boyfriend?"

"No. More like a twin brother. They were BFFs before—" I break off. "It was messy. But Bobby's gone, Nick's girlfriend moved dirt-side, and Nick's alone. The usual sad, holiday story."

We exit the float tubes on Level 6. I'm not sure I want Scott hanging around my compartment, but I really need to change clothes. I could have worn some of the abandoned clothing populating the closets of my room up on 83, but I can't pass up an opportunity to wear my station coverall in front of Mother. It seemed like a good idea this morning, but I'm feeling kind of funky by now.

We swing down the radial to A Ring, and I swipe open the door to our compartment. Loud voices assault our ears as we enter.

"How can you even suggest that?" Kara shrieks. "No one does that!"

"What kind of crazy planet did you grow up on?" Erco screams back. "Everyone does it that way! Your idea is insane!"

"Get out! I can't be with someone who thinks that is okay! Just get out!" Kara flings a shoe at Erco. He leaps out of the way, and it just misses his head.

"Crazy, misguided, backward, idiotic. I can't. I just can't!" He stomps out of the compartment.

Kara bursts into tears. She flings herself at me.

"Go after him," I mouth at Scott over Kara's shoulder. He gives me a nervous look but follows Erco out the door.

Kara and I have been friends a long time, so I know how to deal with this. I hold her for a few minutes, letting her get the first wild sobs out. Then I lead her to the couch and settle her in the corner. Wrapping a blanket around her, I hand her a box of tissues.

"What do you want to drink?" I ask.

With a sniff, she dabs her eyes. "Tea, with rum. Lots of rum."

"Not eggnog?" I ask, thinking of Nicolai.

Kara shudders.

When the tea is ready, I pour in a stiff slug of Cap'n Drake and stir. Plopping down beside her on the couch, I hand her the cup. "What happened?"

Kara's eyes fill with tears, so I hold up a hand. "Whenever you're ready." I flip on a Christmas vid and we watch in silence.

"Okay," I say, when the vid ends. "Do you want to talk about it?"

Kara sniffles and bobbles her head in a non-committal way. She takes a sip of her third cup of tea and pulls the blanket more tightly around her shoulders. Her makeup has smeared, leaving dark circles around her eyes, and tear tracks down her cheeks. "We were talking about Christmas."

We sit in silence for a couple minutes. "And?" I finally prompt when it becomes obvious she isn't continuing.

"And he, I can't believe anyone, he—" She wipes away fresh tears. "This is so hard! I love him so much, but I don't know if I can be with him after this."

"What?!" I squeak. Taking a deep breath, I resist the urge to shake her. "What did he do? Did he cheat on you?"

"No!" she cries, horror on her face. "Why would you think that?"

"Uh, because you're crying, and you said you didn't know if you could stay with him." I get up from the couch to make my own cup of tea. Good thing today isn't a workday because if she keeps up like this, I'm going to start drinking, too.

"No, nothing like that. It's just how can you be with someone whose beliefs are so different from your own?" She blows her nose and takes another gulp of tea.

"Is he super religious? Or an atheist?" During the years we've lived together, Kara has displayed a vague belief in God, but I've seen no active participation in any religion.

"No, it's not religion." She sniffles again and puts her cup down on the table. Taking a deep breath, she flings her arms out dramatically. "He thinks we should have beaf for Christmas dinner!"

My jaw drops. "Beaf?"

"I know!" she exclaims. "How could anyone have beaf for Christmas? It's —it's un-Kakuvian!"

I burst out laughing.

Kara glares. "Stop laughing! This is important! No one on Kaku has beaf for Christmas! No one! Everyone knows you eat tirkey for the holidays! What kind of family does he come from if they eat beaf for Christmas?"

I laugh harder. Finally, eyes streaming, I lean against the counter and grab a tissue. "Kara, if you're looking that hard for an excuse to dump him, just do it already."

"What do you mean? I don't want to dump Erco! I love him. He's the most amazing guy I've ever dated. He makes me feel all warm and squishy. We were talking about registering a contract."

"Really?" I'm shocked. Although I guess I shouldn't be. Kara has dated a lot. Conservatively, I'd estimate about 80 guys in the six years we've been friends. When she's on a roll, she goes through them weekly. And keep in mind she never dated while school was in session, so we're only talking summers during the first four years. She's been with Erco for a couple months.

"I know." She nods. "He's the one. If we can get beyond this beaf thing."

"Kara, honey, I'm not sure how to break this to you." I pause.

"What? Do you think I should dump him? I can't!" she wails.

"No, I think he's perfect for you. You should sign a contract with procreational options and move to Kaku and grow old together." I smile.

"Then what is it?"

"My family has always had beaf for Christmas dinner."

Stunned silence blankets the room. Kara blinks. "What?"

"You heard me. Mother serves beaf for Christmas. Actually, she serves real beef, but close enough. Standing rib roast, usually."

Kara stares at me. "Huh."

I shrug. "Of course, she usually serves turkey, too."

"Real turkey?" Kara asks.

I roll my eyes. "What do you think?"

"Right, of course the Ice Dame has real turkey. And beef. Wow. I had no idea." She wipes her face, smearing her make up even more.

"So, go wash your face, and let's go find Erco." I reach down a hand and pull her up off the couch.

She goes into the bathroom. Water splashes, and the toilet flushes.

A few minutes later, she re-emerges with her makeup perfect again. Kara has always been a pretty crier. No red nose, puffy eyes, or thick voice for her.

"Say…. What did you get Erco for Christmas?"

"Oh, I got him the most amazing thing!" she gushes. "Do you want to see it? I've already wrapped it, but I can show you a holo." She gestures to the corner of the room. A tiny Christmas tree sits on a table by the window. It's about half a meter high, and sparkles with red, green, and gold ornaments and lights. A small pile of wrapped gifts lay scattered below.

"When did you do that?" I ask.

She stares at me. "The tree has been there for a week, but Erco and I decorated it a couple days ago. Didn't you notice it before?"

I shrug. "I haven't been here a lot, you know. I guess I kind of missed it."

"You really don't have to move out when he's here." She flicks her holo-ring and swipes through some screens. "We don't mind if you stay."

I grimace. "That's ok. I've been busy. And I'd rather—" I trail off. "You two get kind of loud, and I don't need to hear all that," I say in a rush.

Kara's eyes widen. "Really? Even with the sound dampers on?"

"You haven't been turning them on. But yeah, even after I turn them on, I can hear way more than I care to. It's not a big deal, though. There are plenty of places for me to stay."

She bites her lip, but I smile and nod emphatically.

"If you're sure," she says. "But you can come back any time. And he won't be here long. He has to go back on duty before New Year's. Anyway, check this out! It's the perfect gift for Erco!" The holo rotates slowly in her palm.

"What is that?" I ask.

"A real Earth leather weightlifting belt and matching gloves." She zooms in. "Look at the gold stitching! And there's Swift-Sure latching technology in the buckle. It even monitors your sweat rate."

"Wow, that's something."

She sighs. "I know. He's going to love it."

"Zark, that doesn't help me at all," I mutter as we leave the compartment.

"What?" Kara squeaks. "Do you mean you haven't gotten a gift for Ty, yet?"

I hang my head. "No, I didn't even think about it until yesterday. I've never had a significant other at holiday time before."

"Triana, that's so sad!" Kara flings an arm around me as we walk up the radial. "Christmas gifts are one of the best things about dating! Well, that and sex, of course." She smiles, smugly.

I glare at her. "You know we aren't there."

She just shakes her head. "What are you waiting for?"

I'm saved from answering by our arrival in the concourse. The sound hits us like a wall as we step out of the radial. It looks like yesterday's party down on Level 2 had babies and invited all their friends over. Except these are adults, not children. Actually, very few people choose to raise their kids on the station. Most families move dirt-side during the child-rearing years. But I digress.

A sea of yelling, drinking, dancing, and singing bodies fills the space. Everyone who lives on this level must be out here. Bad Christmas music blares through the room. Jugs, cups, and bottles get passed hand to hand, even though it's not even lunchtime. Someone fires off a popper, and confetti flies through the air. I wince. My bots will be working overtime this week.

We follow Kara's holo-ring to Level 18. The atmosphere here is frantic, full of people rushing from shop to shop, dragging double handfuls of bags and boxes. We find Erco and Scott at a small coffee shop off C Ring. Erco spots us from their small table next to the windows. His chair crashes over backward as he springs to his feet and races out the door. Kara throws herself at him, crying again.

I skirt the happy couple and join Scott at the table. "Can you believe them? They nearly broke up over chicken or beef."

"Turkey or beef." Scott raises his mug in salute. "Who would eat chicken for Christmas?"

I snort. "Yeah, I didn't dare tell her the Ice Dame also serves fish."

Scott laughs. "Is that tonight's menu? My waistband already feels tighter."

"Oh, tonight will have more options than you can imagine. She pulls out ALL the stops for the SK'Corp holiday party."

"I don't know." Scott shakes his head. "I can imagine a lot. So, what are you going to get your boyfriend for Christmas."

"What?" I yelp.

He rolls his eyes. "It was obvious last night that you hadn't gotten him anything. I can help. It's my superpower."

"Right," I say dryly. "Your superpower is saving Christmas."

"Of course." He smiles.

SEVEN

WE'VE JUST REACHED the swanky shops on Level 67 when my holo-ring buzzes. The upper levels are even more frantic than the lower ones, with long lines and rabid shoppers ripping items from each other's hands. The low-key jazz carols are nearly inaudible, drowned out by screeching and yelling. A layer of sweat and desperation mixes badly with the peppermint air freshener, leaving me a little queasy.

"I need to take this," I tell Scott, stepping into a quiet radial.

Scott follows me down the hall to a bot duct, which I open, and we scoot inside. "This is much nicer than where we met," Scott jokes. "Next time I get amnesia, I'm doing it up here."

I roll my eyes and accept the call. The holo of a slender man with straight dark hair, almond-shaped eyes and a hooked nose pops up in my palm. "Good morning, Hy-Mi."

"Is it?" Hy-Mi's usually serene face sports a sheen of sweat, and his eyes are bloodshot and wild. "Is it a good morning, Sera? I wouldn't know—I haven't had a good night's sleep in weeks."

I glance at Scott, then look back at my palm. I've never heard Hy-Mi sound so frantic. "What's wrong?"

"That woman is going to drive me to drink! Or out an airlock!" Hy-Mi breathes heavily.

"Is Gloria messing with you, too?" I ask.

"Gloria? The kitchen intern? She isn't helping. But I meant your Mother!" He spits the words out like an unripe pestimmon.

"What did she do? I've never seen you so ruffled!"

"She's never been so unreasonable. So capricious! So gauche." His eyes flick off screen, then back. He leans in close. "This morning, she decided to change all the party favors. Two hundred of them. She does that all the time, although rarely so close to show time. But today she demanded—" He looks upward and drops his voice. "She demanded stockings."

"Stockings?"

"Yes, red stockings with fuzzy white tops!" His lip curls as if he can smell Nicolai Bezos from across the level. "With 'stuffers' inside! I don't even know what that means!"

Scott steps forward. "I think that might be my fault. When we were talking about Christmas traditions this morning, I mentioned stockings. Usually they're hung by the chimney with care."

I stare at Scott. "With care?"

He nods solemnly. "Yes, with care. But tiny ones would make fun party favors. Hy-Mi, why don't you let me and Triana handle the stockings? I'm sure you have more pressing things to do."

Hy-Mi draws himself up to his full height—which isn't impressive and is truly adorable when viewed via a palm-sized holo—and bows. "Thank you, Ser Calvin. This is most generous of you. I'm so sorry to have troubled you."

Scott waves a hand. "No problem at all! I'm a Christmas expert."

After Hy-Mi signs off, I look at Scott. "Stockings? Where are we going to get those?"

He smiles. "It's my superpower."

THREE HOURS LATER, we're back up on 83 with more bags and packages than we can carry. Station retailers delivered them to Rafe's desk, but they can't come up to 83. Scott and I make three trips up the lift tube.

We've laid everything out in Mother's yoga studio. A pile of small red stockings lays in one corner. Scott found them in the back of a tiny store I didn't even know existed down on Level 13. They had exactly two hundred of them. What kind of crazy luck is that?

A zillion different piles of tiny treasures encircle us. All of them are wrapped in bright Christmas paper. I don't know how he convinced the vendors to wrap them, but they all happily complied. And none of them charged us for the extra work.

Scott hands me a detailed schematic, sketched out on a shopping bag. "If we stuff the stockings according to these plans, each one will contain a unique combination of gifts."

I shake my head. "Christmas really is your superpower."

LIKE ALL OF Mother's parties, this one sparkles. Wealthy people in designer clothing, drinking exclusive cocktails, nibbling exotic foods. The silver and green theme of the living room extends through the formal parlor and the dining room. The holographic flames of long silver candles reflect off brilliant white china, silver, and crystal covering the tables. The red stockings in the center of each place setting provide a splash of contrasting color, and the effect is stunning.

"Your stockings look fabulous, Ser Calvin." Hy-Mi straightens one. His formal tunic matches the dark green and silver of the room. "You are a miracle worker."

I laugh. "You don't believe in miracles, Hy-Mi."

Hy-Mi glares at me. Scott smiles and bows in reply. He looks fantastic in an old-fashioned black tuxedo with a red tie and vest. I'm wearing a close-fitting, full-length black gown with a moderate neckline and a slit up to my mid-thigh. I haven't worn anything so slinky in a long time.

The guests circulate through the room, ooh-ing and ah-ing about the tiny gifts spilling out of each stocking. Mother will live on this triumph for weeks.

"Bogie at ten o'clock," I whisper to Hy-Mi.

"What's a bogie?" Scott asks. "And it's only eight."

"It's an ancient Earth military thing. It means, 'look out, there's a bad guy.' I'm not sure what the time has to do with it." I jerk my chin at the front room.

Nicolai Bezos has just entered. He's accompanied by one of the Zuckerberg twins—I'm not sure which one since they're identical. I give Hy-Mi a nod and steer Scott out of the dining room on an intercept course. "Nick has a history of arriving completely blotto. He drinks so much, the Buzzkill in the food can't come close to compensating."

But today Nick looks sober. His gait is steady, his eyes are clear, his smile is pleasant. And the Zuckerbergs are both serious, studious, non-partying girls. The fact that one of them came with Nick is unprecedented.

Nick spots us and heads our direction. "Ser Calvin," he says as they approach. "I'd like you to meet my companion, Zerina Zuckerberg." He clears his throat. "I owe you a sincere thank you. I don't know what you did, but—" He breaks off. "This sounds so stupid, but I think you fixed me. When we met in the lobby I was trashed, and by the time you got me home, I'd decided to make a change. I haven't had a drink all day, which is a miracle for me."

Scott waves him off. "I didn't do anything. It's all you, my friend. I hope you stay clean." He claps Nick on the shoulder and smiles at his date as they move away to greet the Buffetts. Scott pulls my arm through his, steering me toward the kitchen.

"There's that word again," I say. "Christmas miracles really are your business, apparently."

Scott snorts. "How would I make a guy sober up? It's all in his imagination."

"Why are we going to the kitchen?"

"I'm not sure." Scott waves the door open and we step in. "I just feel the need to be here."

The door opens onto a butler's pantry. We duck out of the way as men and women in formal attire stride in and out, like clockwork. They pick up trays of food and drink as they depart, and deposit empties when they return. The full trays slide out of automated doors above the counter. The empties go into a bin that disappears through another hatch when full.

We wait for a lull, then dart across the space and into the kitchen proper.

The noise is deafening. Pans and utensils clatter, people yell, pots boil. A dozen white-coated chefs work at stations around the room, stirring and dishing. An amazing aroma wafts around us—a mix of roasting meats, fresh bread, spiced cakes, rich sauces, and of course, chocolate. My stomach growls, loudly. Scott's answers, and he chuckles.

Dav directs the controlled chaos, roaming the room, tasting, seasoning, rearranging. His usually clean white coat is smeared, and his hat sits precariously on his head. Someone drops something, and he whips around, assessing the damage.

I take a deep lungful of the delicious air and smile at Scott. "Looks pretty standard to me. I used to sneak down here during parties when I was young. Dav would always find a task for me and feed me dessert after the mad rush. This kitchen is one of my favorite places."

We make ourselves as small as possible, standing against a wall near the door. Around the corner, a team arranges hors-d'oeuvres on trays before they disappear through the delivery hatch. Gloria stands behind them, watching. One of the men demands over his shoulder, "I need another tray."

Gloria grits her teeth and hands him a tray.

He hands it back. "That's not clean. Get me another. And, wash this one."

Gloria's nostrils flare, but she bites back whatever was on the tip of her tongue and gets another tray. I can't believe the restraint she's showing. She must really hate being relegated to dishwashing.

"Is that another of your Christmas miracles?" I ask Scott.

"How would I do that?" He puts his index fingers to his temples. "Mind control?"

We watched an old vid while we stuffed stockings earlier. The story featured a villain who could control others telepathically, and his eventual, fitting demise. Not really Christmas fare, but it was good fun.

"I hope not," I say. "That never works out."

Scott steps forward, picking up a small jar on the counter. "What's this?" He looks around the room. No one pays any attention. A short man next to him pounds something in a huge pot. On the far side of the counter, two more white-clad men roll and fold some kind of pastry dough. A distracted woman carrying a huge, gray tub of dirty dishes reaches out and takes the jar from Scott.

"De Meyer! What is that? Did you put something in the potatoes?" Dav's voice rings across the room. He's pointing at the woman. The mashing man turns to look, surprise on his face.

The woman freezes. "I didn't touch the potatoes, Chef," she says. "I'm just collecting dirty dishes for the intern to wash."

Out of the corner of my eye, I see a small movement. I turn quickly, zeroing in on Gloria, but she continues to wash dishes, completely focused on her task.

Which is totally suspicious. Gloria hard at work? Besides, she loves conflict. She'd normally be all over De Meyer. But, I swear I saw just the tiniest smirk on her lips. What has she done?

Dav grabs the jar and sniffs it. Then he looks into the pot on the counter. It's full of creamy white mashed potatoes. He smells the potatoes, and his eyes narrow. He straightens up and stares around the room, watching. After a moment, his eyes snag on mine. He gives some low instructions to the man with the masher. The man questions, then agrees.

As Dav turns to us, the man behind him throws the masher into the pot and lugs it away.

Dav stops next to me, turning to face the room. His eyes travel around it, watching, weighing. Without looking in my in direction, he hands me the jar and mutters, "Do you still have that analyzer?"

I wrinkle my nose. When I was a teen, I created an app that scanned food for foreign particles. It was only marginally successful at doing its job. The project was spectacularly successful at inducing food poisoning, however, as I attempted to test my creation on unwary guests.

"I have a better option." I pull up the surveillance cams and roll back in time. Sure enough, Gloria poured the contents of the jar into the potatoes. "Make her eat some."

Dav looks scandalized. Scott bursts out laughing. His deep chuckles draw attention from the entire staff. I catch Gloria's eyes and smile. Her eyes widen then narrow. She whips back around to the dish sink.

"Intern!" Dav roars.

Gloria straightens slowly and turns. "Yes, Chef?" A sweet smile is plastered on her face. With quick, graceful steps, she crosses the kitchen to us.

"Taste the potatoes," Dav barks.

Color drains from her cheeks. "I, uh, I'm on a low carb diet." Her eyes dart to the man approaching with the massive potato pot. "Even a tiny bite will throw me out of ketogenisis."

"Ketosis," Dav says.

"What?" Gloria asks.

"What, Chef." Dav snaps.

Gloria's voice wavers. "What, Chef?"

"The word you're looking for is ketosis. Which you'd know if you needed to follow that diet. Taste the potatoes." His face is bland, but his voice is like iron.

Gloria stares at Dav for a full thirty seconds. Then she whips off her hat and throws it to the ground. "I don't need this! I'm sick of your orders, you pathetic, little man. You'll pay for treating me like this!" She stomps on the hat. A gasp goes up around us.

Gloria shoves past Dav and runs into a brick wall. Or rather, a wall of chefs. "No one talks to Chef Dav like that," De Meyer says. The wall takes a step forward.

"The help leaves through the back," the potato man says, pointing to the staff exit. "Dame Morgan insists."

Gloria's eyes narrow down to mean little slits, but the white wall of chefs takes another step forward, blocking access to the dining room.

"You'll be sorry! You'll all be sorry," Gloria hisses. She flings herself across the room, grabbing the handle of a large saucepan.

Iron fingers close around her wrist. "I wouldn't do that," Scott says pleasantly. "Allow me to escort you out." He leans down and whispers something in her ear.

Gloria looks up at Scott, and her eyes widen. She straightens her shoulders. "Thank you, but that's not necessary. I can find my way out." She pulls her arm from his grasp and stalks to the staff exit.

As the door shuts behind her, a cheer goes up throughout the kitchen. Dav allows his staff to whoop for a few seconds, then claps his hands. "Back to work! We have a meal to prepare." He turns to me and Scott. "Thank you, both. Sera Annabelle, would you check your cams to make sure she didn't taint anything else?" I nod, and he rushes away shouting orders.

Gloria is a one-trick pony—she only adulterated the potatoes. I scroll back carefully, but the chefs were canny enough to keep her away from the rest of the food. She must have messed with enough dishes over the last few weeks to make them all wary. Even the temporary staff seem to have her number. It's a wonder she managed to get to the potatoes.

"I'm going to take this jar down to medical and see if they can tell us what was in it," I tell Scott. "Maybe I can take a scoop of the potatoes, too." We locate the little man emptying the big pot at the rear of the room. I scoop some into another jar and almost lick my finger, it smells so good.

Scott lays a hand on my arm. "Bad idea. Let's go back to the party."

Dav zips over and takes the jars from me. "I'll put these in my office for later. Thanks for saving the party, Sera." He hands me a small plate with a couple confections on it. This man knows me well.

I offer one of the candies to Scott and pop the other in my mouth. My eyes widen. "You're a genius," I whisper through the sweet, creamy, intense flavor. "I love you."

Dav smiles and shoos us out of his kitchen.

"Now you know my kryptonite," I say to Scott.

"I'm no super villain—I use my powers only for good."

I look at him, considering. "How did you know we needed to go into the kitchen at that exact moment?"

He shrugs. "I told you, I had a feeling. I've been worried about her since yesterday. Tonight would have been a perfect opportunity to sabotage so many things."

"What did you say to her? It really seemed to scare her," I dodge a waiter with an empty tray and step back out into the dining room.

Scott follows me, laughing. "I just told her bad girls and boys don't get any Christmas presents."

The rest of the party proceeds normally. Which is to say, it's spectacular, like all Mother's events. The food is fantastic, and Dav even managed to replace the tainted potatoes. Tiny, crispy works of art, piped from potatoes and browned to perfection, grace each plate. The man is another miracle worker.

A waiter offers dozens of desserts. Guests can choose as many as they wish. I order a tasting plate of everything. Gold-dusted chocolate cake, five flavors of pie, tiramisu, flan, custard, cookies, chocolates, cheesecake—a huge tray covered in bite-sized plates arrives at my place, and I dig in.

Scott moves a spoon toward a tiny pink mochi. I narrow my eyes at him. "Don't even think about it, Christmas boy. You have your own."

Scott gazes at me with those huge blue eyes then looks down at his empty plate. "But it's all gone," he whispers.

I relent. "But only half. I want to taste everything."

After the mochi, Scott leans back in his chair while I finish off my desserts. "Where is everyone?"

"What do you mean?" I lick chocolate mousse off a spoon and look around the table. "This is everyone. Well, everyone except Gloria, and she couldn't come because she was 'working'." I make air quotes with my free hand.

"We stuffed two hundred stockings. And yesterday Dav said he was making two hundred figgy puddings. Which I haven't seen yet, by the way." He gestures to the table. "There are only thirty people here."

I snort and dig into an apple tart. "These are the cream of SK'Corp. The board of directors and their favored few. The other hundred and seventy employees of the station have their own parties. Mother made a brief appearance at each one earlier tonight. But she doesn't allow the rabble up here." I shrug. "To be fair, there isn't room for everyone. And some of them are still on duty anyway. We can hit the Ops party later if you want. It will be way more fun. But the food isn't as good."

Scott waves a lazy hand. "I leave it up to you. You're the expert."

EIGHT

WHEN DINNER IS FINISHED, Don Gates decides to regale the group with his rendition of *Christmas on Andromeda*. He had a good voice when he was young, or so I'm told, but he's closing in on eighty-five and the rejuv doesn't do as good a job on voices as it does on faces.

Scanning the room for Scott, I slide toward the foyer. As I reach the threshold, I spot him, listening to Dame Zuckerberg. My shoulders slump. We'll never get out of here—that woman can talk! Scott catches my eye and makes a shooing motion with his fingers. When Dame Z glances away, he mouths, "Save yourself." Not wanting his self-sacrifice to be in vain, I slip out the door.

The Ops party takes place in the multi-grav gym down on Level 6. I can feel the music vibrating the deck before I reach the door. When it whooshes open, I'm assaulted by pounding drums, wailing guitars and a breathy voice singing about "sexy Santa." I immediately visualize a pudgy man in red, fur-trimmed bikini briefs, making pouty faces, and I burst into laughter.

A few folks turn at the sound and wave but return to their conversations. I say hello to some friends and grab a drink just to have something in my hand. My stomach is so full, I couldn't possibly put anything else into it. I circulate through the party, nodding and waving, but not stopping to talk to anyone.

I stop in a corner near the door, leaning against the wall. I watch the dancers in their ugly Christmas shirts and the grungy looking band wearing tinsel and bows over their torn jeans and ratty t-shirts. I'm just not feeling it, tonight. Setting the still-full glass down on a side table, I slide out the door again. Escaping two parties in one night is far from a record for me.

Outside the gym, I consider my options. I can go back up to the penthouse and try to sneak into my room without getting busted. If I use a maintenance corridor, it should be doable, but the thought of being trapped in the gilt castle is not attractive. I can go back to my compartment, but a quick check of my illegal tracking app shows me Kara and Erco are already there.

I could go to O'Neill's compartment, but I don't like being there when he's not around. It feels invasive and lonely.

I wander through the mostly deserted radials and rings, feeling kind of sorry for myself. Having a boyfriend means I shouldn't be alone on Christmas, right? A tiny voice tells me it's not Christmas yet, and I could be enjoying one of the many parties, but I tell the tiny voice to shut up and let me mope.

I find myself in one of my favorite spots on the station. A Ring on Level 20 is a farm space, full of green and growing fruits and vegetables. It's closed to the public, but as a maintenance tech, I can get in. I push through the foliage and make my way to the break room.

This breakroom is a well-kept secret. I discovered it shortly after I arrived on station, when I realized my cleaning bots were avoiding it. In exchange for promising to keep their secret, the farm crew allow me to hang out here whenever I like. I push open the door and step into the hidden glen.

They've transformed their break room into a magical clearing. Thick plants grow around the edges, hiding the walls. A tiny fountain provides the sound of running water. A small hill slopes down to the external windows, allowing you to lay on the grass and watch the sunrise. I glance at my station schedule—this side of the station is turned away from the sun and won't rotate around until early morning. But that's ok—deep space fits my mood tonight.

I lay back on the hill and gaze at the stars.

"Excuse me." A high voice breaks into my solitude. It's clear and beautiful, like a musical instrument, but not one I've ever heard before. "Can you help me?"

I roll up on an elbow. "Who are you?"

A small woman stands just inside the door. She's really tiny—maybe only a meter tall. Although I've seen little people on vids, I've never seen one in person. I think they've been genetically manipulated out of existence, at least in the higher tech areas of the galaxy. So much for diversity! Just edit it out.

The woman steps forward. "I'm Mary." She's dressed mostly in red and tiny silver bells jingle on the hems of her skirt and blouse. "I'm looking for... something we've lost."

"Okaaay. Who are 'we' and what have you lost? And how did you end up in here? This section is restricted."

Mary shrugs. "The door opened, and I came in. That happens sometimes, when it's the right place."

"What?" I narrow my eyes. "Have you been drinking too much eggnog?"

She smiles, and a feeling of joy and contentment wafts over me. "There's no such thing as too much eggnog!" She giggles.

I sit up. "Sure, sure. Who did you say you are?"

"I'm Mary. We're just visiting here. Or we will be. But we've lost something, and you can help us find it."

"One of us has clearly drunk too much eggnog, no matter what you say." I rub my temples. "What did you lose?" Based on her clothing and stature, Mary is not local. She must be from one of the ships docked on Level 40. I get to my feet. "Why don't we see if we can get you back to your ship?"

"Thanks," Mary says, "but I know where my ship is. I don't want to go there right now. I need to find what we lost."

I take a deep breath. "If you would just tell me what you're looking for, I can help you find it."

She looks me in the eyes, and that feeling of contentment settles over me again. Her golden-brown eyes seem to expand and wrap around me. I could get completely lost in them. With a start, I find myself back on my butt, on the hill.

"You'll help us when the time is right. See you soon!" She steps away into the thick brush.

I start to tell her the door is behind the palm tree, but it seems like too much effort. She'll find it eventually. If she got in here, she knows how to get out. I lean back against the warm grass and gaze at the stars.

A SPLASH of water gets me right in the face. My eyes fly open, just in time to take a second assault. Forking sprinklers!

Scrambling to my feet, I dodge the spray. Sunlight dances on the water, dazzling my eyes. It must be early morning.

I duck between the ferns and look for the door. It's exactly where I remembered—behind the small palm. I wonder if the tiny woman is still back there, lost, and realize it had to have been a dream. Wiping water from my face, I make my way up to Level 83.

AFTER A SHOWER AND FRESH CLOTHES, I find Scott eating waffles in the dining room. He's wearing another red sweater and faded jeans. His hair is still damp, and a fine blond stubble fuzzes his cheek.

"You growing a beard?" I ask.

Scott smiles and raises a glass of orange juice to me, his mouth full. He chews, swallows, and takes a gulp of juice. "Busy day today!" He cuts another chunk of waffle with his fork.

"Really?" Grabbing a plate, I cruise the buffet. As always, Dav has provided a huge selection of pastries and breakfast foods. It seems like a waste for only two or three people, but anything we don't eat goes to the company cafeteria on Level 20. Sometimes I think the Ice Dame's leftovers feed half the station.

I pile strawberries on my own waffle, and spoon on a dollop of whipped cream. "Did you remember who you are and why you're here?"

He waves that off as if it's not important. "It's Christmas Eve! We still have a present to buy!" He shoves a whole piece of bacon into his mouth.

"And it's Sunday. We should start with church. Best way to start the week."

I look at him in surprise. Somehow, I had mentally classified him as a spacer—someone who lives on a ship. Those guys are frequently religious. Some of them even cult-like. But few ships have clergy or a regular worship schedule, so going to Sunday church—or Saturday temple, or Friday mosque—is not usually on their radar.

"Okay, there are services at the Sanctuary all morning. Take your pick." I pull a schedule from the OS and throw it up on the screen above the buffet.

AFTER THE SERVICE, Scott links his arm through mine, and we wander out into the concourse. "You're still looking for something special for Ty, right?" Scott asks.

I blink, surprised he remembered O'Neill's first name. "Yeah," I say slowly, but I feel less frantic about it for some reason. Maybe some lingering effect of that weird dream last night. An echo of that feeling of safety and contentment washes over me again. "We have to find your ship, too."

"How do you know I have a ship?" he asks absently, gazing in a store window.

"You're obviously not from here, but you got here somehow. I haven't found any record of you on any of the shuttles up from Kaku." I tick the items off on my fingers as we walk. "None of the cruise ships currently docked have flagged anyone missing. They keep pretty close count on anyone who comes on-station. None of the recently departed ships have posted anyone missing, either. You're listed in the OS as a VIP visitor, so you must have arrived on a private vessel from out-system."

"That is pretty compelling." Scott leads the way down a radial. "What's down here?"

We wander the inner rings of the mid-levels for a couple hours, but nothing screams O'Neill's name at me. At midday, we stop at the Lunch Alley on Level 24. Tiny pushcarts line a section of B Ring, offering exotic foods and beverages. We take our meal and head to the park on Level 25. Gazing out at the stars, we eat in silence.

Scott sits back with a sigh, wiping some sauce off his beard. I do a double take. "You have the fastest growing beard I've ever seen! Did Kara talk you into some new growth accelerator?"

He rubs a hand over his centimeter-long facial hair, shaking his head. "That's crazy. It didn't grow this fast yesterday. One of life's unsolved mysteries. Tell me about Ty O'Neill."

"What? Why?"

"You want to get him a gift." Scott runs a hand through his platinum hair, pushing it off his face. "He's obviously important to you. Finding the perfect gift means understanding the relationship. So, tell me about him."

"He works for board security."

"I know where he works. Are you in love?" His blue eyes bore into mine.

I gulp. "I, uh, he's not, we don't—"

Scott waves a hand. "Got it. Not ready for the L word. What do you two like to do together?"

What *do* we like to do together? I'm not sure. We've been too busy saving the galaxy to do things we like. "Uh, watch vids? Eat pizza? Hack into computer systems and stop bad guys? You ask some hard questions."

"Let's try this a different way." He stands up and gestures for me to walk with him. We cross a miniature bridge over a tiny trickle of water. "Why him? Why do you want to get a gift for Ty O'Neill? Why not, say, Nick Bezos? Now that he's sober, he seems to be a good guy."

We walk in silence as I ponder that question. My first reaction was to say, "Because he's my boyfriend. Sort of." But I think Scott is looking for something deeper than that. Like: *why* is Ty O'Neill my sort of boyfriend?

We leave the park and walk inward, toward the concourse. "He gets me," I finally say. "He knows both sides of my identity, and he understands, now, why I left all that." I wave a hand at the ceiling, indicating the upper levels of the station. "He knows I like *Ancient TēVē*, and he doesn't make fun of it. He knows that I'm an introvert, and even though he isn't, he respects my need for solitude. He appreciates my tech skills and doesn't feel threatened when I'm smarter than him. He loves his family, and knows I love mine, even when I don't like them very much."

As we take the float tube up, I think about all that. It's all true. A warm feeling spreads through my stomach and chest. This is getting way too real.

I'm not ready for the L word, and I'm certainly not going to say it to Scott first!

When we step out, I look at Scott. "Plus, he's really hot."

Scott laughs. And I'd swear his beard is even longer. His eyes twinkle.

I look around. "Why are we on 40? There are only duty-free shops here."

Scott shakes his head. "This is where I need to be." He strides away down Radial 4, slaloming around the occasional pedestrian.

I run to catch up, almost barreling into a woman with a toddler. I dodge around her and grab Scott's arm. "What do you mean? Is this like the kitchen? Are you going to perform another Christmas miracle?"

Scott doesn't answer. He pats my hand and walks to the end of the radial, stopping at a gate. Beyond the gate, the transit arms lead out to the passenger ship docks. People mill around, waiting for ships to arrive or depart. He looks at them, his eyes searching. Then he shrugs. "I guess we'll just wait."

"Wait for what?" I ask.

"Her." He nods.

I turn and follow his gaze. He's looking through the gate at the people in the transit arm. Half a dozen people wander around and I can't tell who he's talking about.

"Who?" I ask.

A feeling of peace comes over me. A high voice, soft and clear cuts through the din, like a ringing bell. "San—Captain! Here you are!" I look down, knowing who I'll see: Mary, the tiny woman from my dream.

"Y— you're real?" I stutter. She smiles, and I feel such a rush of content-ment that I don't care if she answers or not.

"Thank you for finding San—I mean, Captain Calvin for us."

Scott stares at her, blinking, and recognition flashes across his face.

"I, uh, you're welcome. Who are you?"

She smiles again.

"Stop that!" I say. "Tell me what's going on!"

Scott and Mary exchange a look. "She's pretty strong-willed," Mary says.

"I know," Scott nods then turns to me. "Look, I can't tell you things you already know. So just accept what you suspect is true, and you'll be right."

I level a look at him. "Really? You're going all woo-woo on me?"

109

He looks at Mary again. She shrugs. He turns back to me. "My name really is Scott Calvin. And yes, before you ask, I really did have amnesia. I'm still not sure how I ended up on SK2. But you found me, and took care of me, and helped me share Christmas joy. And you helped me find Mary, and my ship."

"I didn't help you—you found Mary all by yourself. I followed you here, remember?" I fling a hand back the way we came.

"But I wouldn't have gotten here without you. Or at least, I would have been a lot lonelier while I was searching." He reaches over the gate, and Mary hands him a small package.

"But you helped us," I protest. "You helped Mother with her party favors, and her gift for R'ger, and saved Dav from the horrible Gloria, and helped me bring Kara and Erco back together. And you bought me lunch." I feel pressure in my eyes, and I blink madly.

Scott smiles and presses the package into my hands. "We spread lots of Christmas spirit together. That's always a good thing. But now Mary and I have to get back to the ship and the crew. We have a lot of deliveries to make. Merry Christmas, Triana." He leans in, smelling like gingerbread and cocoa, and kisses me on the cheek. And then he's gone.

I blink. He and Mary are gone. Just poof, as if they never existed. I look down at the package in my hands. It's plain brown paper, with words scrawled on it in black ink: "Open now. Don't wait for Christmas."

I RACE BACK DOWN to Level 6 and burst into our compartment. Setting the package carefully on a counter, I dash to my specially wired console and log into the OS.

"What's going on?" Kara looks up from her magazine. Sitting next to her on the couch, Erco ignores me, focused on some sports event on his holo.

I pull up the list of ships docked at SK2. There are slips for eight ships on Arm 4. Six are listed as currently empty. A cruise ship is pulling away—they undocked an hour ago—long before Scott and Mary disappeared. The last slip holds a small, independent transport that docked last night. They're getting ready to depart.

"Got you," I mutter, worming into the port data.

"Got who?" Kara gets up and stands beside me, looking at the screen.

"Scott." I stab at an icon. "He's leaving with a tiny woman on this ship." I stab at the icon.

"You know you sound crazy, right?" She puts a hand on my arm.

"It's right outside!" I race to the wall of windows on the far side of the room. I put my hands and nose against the plasglass and look up. More than thirty levels above us, the transit arm sticks out into space. Beyond the slender arm, the massive cruiser crawls away from the station.

On this side, seeming to hang from the arm by an access tube, a shiny red ship glitters in the sun that's just appearing around the edge of the station. It's a sleek little ship with eight engines and rows of bright white lights.

As we watch, the ship detaches from the access tube. It drops toward us, gracefully cutting through space.

"Ops is going to go supernova," Kara says as the ship swoops toward the station.

"Why aren't the proximity alarms going?" I wonder, staring at the ship.

As it approaches, the sunlight glints off the gold trim on the hull, picking out the name: *Reinsdyr*. It swings by, like a fighter plane buzzing the tower in one of those *Ancient TēVē* vids. And although there's no way I can possibly see that far, I'd swear I see Scott and Mary waving at me through the window. It swoops away.

I drop into the armchair.

Erco looks up. "Hey, Tree, what's up?"

I am NOT going to tell Erco what just happened.

"We just saw Santa!" Kara cries, flinging herself down next to Erco.

He stares at her. "You saw Santa."

"You did, too! Scott Calvin—he's Santa! And he gave Triana a present!"

"What are you talking about?" He turns to me. "What is she talking about?"

I explain about the *Reinsdyr*, the tiny woman named Mary, and Scott's magically growing beard.

Kara bounces up and down on the couch. "Really? An elf? I thought he was Santa even before I heard about the elf!"

I look at her. "You did? Why?"

"You've heard the song Sexy Santa, right?! It describes Scott perfectly. And when I saw his beard this morning—"

I interrupt her. "When did you see him this morning?"

"He posted a selfie on the station net." She flicks her holo-ring and brings up *InstaShare*. There's a picture of me and Scott, sitting in the park on Level 25. When did he take that? *How* did he take that? He doesn't have a holo-ring.

"He looks just like the song says! Bright blue, twinkling eyes, white hair, tight abs." She smiles.

"That is not how I picture Santa," Erco says. "But I'm a hetero dude, so…."

"Open your present, Triana!" Kara leaps up and grabs the package, shoving it at me.

I pull the old-fashioned twine, and the brown paper falls away. Inside are two smaller packages. One is wrapped in red and gold striped paper and tied with narrow gold string. The other has shiny blue wrapping with stars scattered over it and a wide silver ribbon. The blue one has a small, silver card that says "Triana."

I open the card.

> My Dear Triana,
>
> Thank you for taking me in and making me part of your
> family. You truly live the Spirit of Christmas. Please accept
> this small token from me and the crew. And I've included
> something special you can give to Ty. Trust me, he'll
> love it.
>
> SC

"SC." I run a finger over the initials. "Scott Calvin."

"Santa Claus!" Kara cries. "Open the gift. Open the gift!"

"You'll just have to wait until Ty gets here." I hold it out of reach.

As if in response to my statement, the doorbell rings. I jump up and wave the door open, and there he is. Like magic.

"Hey," I say.

"Hey, yourself." He slides an arm around me and gives me a kiss that curls my toes.

Someone pulls my arm. I open my eyes. Kara drags me away from the door. "Open the gifts! Open the gifts!"

"Calm down, Kara!" Erco laughs. He pushes her down on the couch and goes to the kitchen corner. "You two want some mulled wine?"

With our drinks at hand, we settle down into the chairs. I throw a fireplace vid up on the big screen. Kara hands me the red and gold package and explains to Ty about Scott, the red spaceship, the tiny woman.

"This guy is buying gifts for my girl?" Ty asks. "Should I be worried?'

"Aren't you listening?" Kara cries. "He's Santa!"

"It's for you." I hand the package to Ty.

"Really? You didn't have to get me a gift." He turns the small package around in his hands, looking at the beautiful wrapping.

"I didn't. Scott did. Oh, just open it already!"

He snaps the gold string and unwraps the box. He looks inside, and glances up at me, puzzled.

I raise my eyebrows.

He shrugs. Reaching inside, he pulls out a small glass sphere. It sits comfortably in the palm of his hand. He holds it up to the light. "I'm not sure what this is."

"It's a vid globe." I reach forward to take it from him. "I've never seen one outside a museum or, well, a vid." I hand it back to him.

"How does it work?" Kara leans over the back of Ty's chair.

"This says they haven't been made in over a hundred years." I scroll through a wiki page on my holo-ring. "Squeeze it, gently, to activate it."

A cone of light pops up from the sphere in Ty's hand. It glows blue then brightens to white. A still picture of me appears in the cone. Then it swirls and transforms into a picture of me and Ty. We watch, mesmerized, as a parade of pictures and short vids from my personal files appear in succession. How did Scott get them onto that sphere? Maybe he really is magic.

"It's beautiful! I love it." Ty sets it carefully on the table and pulls me into his arms for a tender kiss.

"Open the other one!" Kara cries, bringing us back to reality.

I laugh and take the blue box from her. I pull off the ribbon and carefully unwrap the box. Normally, I'd just rip the paper off, but this wrapping is exquisite. Setting it aside, I open the box. Inside is a crystal bowl with a lid. I pull it out. And start laughing.

It's chocolate. And not just any chocolate. "These are Dav's chocolates. How did Scott get them? And when did he write that note?" Mary brought this package to him at the gate.

"Christmas magic," Kara breathes.

I offer the candy to the others. There are eight beautiful chocolates, and we each take one. Setting the bowl down on the table, I notice something else inside the box. I pull out a small card and burst out laughing again.

"What?" Kara asks.

I hold it up. "It's a delivery invoice for a Vacu-Bot 5001 with Tinsel Busting Technology. Santa really knows the way to a Space Janitor's heart!"

IF YOU ENJOYED THIS STORY, consider signing up for my newsletter. I have another *Space Janitor Christmas* story available exclusively to newsletter subscribers, plus several other free stories. And I'll let you know when I publish more *Space Janitor* stories.

Speaking of that, there's a full list of my currently available books on the next page.

CHRISTMAS ON KAKU

ANOTHER SPACE JANITOR CHRISTMAS STORY

I'VE NEVER SPENT Christmas on a planet before.

I grew up on Station Kelly Kornienko, which orbits high above the planet Kaku. Everything about SK2 is sanitized and packaged to keep the wealthy people on the upper levels happy. The upper-levs, as we call them, pay a premium for this.

But Kaku is different. Everywhere I look, there are bright lights, tacky decorations, and fake snow. These people have obviously never experienced real snow—their version looks like cotton puffs and spray-on whipped topping.

I kick a stray puff off the path and continue past Luberick Center toward the dorms. It's the end of exam week at the Turing-Sassoon Technology Institute of Esthetics and Computing — Kaku. Or as we like to call it, the TechnoInst. I'm done. Exhausted.

I walk past a construction zone and around the hedges on the far side. The older residence stacks—res-stacks—are a zillion clicks from the rest of the campus, and I'm too broke to take a robo-taxi. I trudge across the thick grass, the hot sun weighing on me like a blanket. Most of the time I don't mind it, but Christmas is supposed to be cold, right?

"Triana! Triana Moore!"

I spin around. "Hey, Kara. Are you headed back to the dorm?"

"No, I need your help," she says, grabbing my arm. She flashes her bright smile and pulls me back toward the main campus. "Your roots are showing, and I need a victim, I mean, client."

My hand flies to my head. "My roots?"

She shrugs, and her whole body shimmers in the skin-tight cat suit she's wearing today. It's shiny red, with black and white graphics printed to look like an elf costume. The low-cut neckline reveals a wide expanse of cleavage, and the tight belt emphasizes her tiny waist and large booty. I push my envy down, deep inside my not-curvy body.

"Yeah," she says. "I noticed some red this morning. Are you going natural?" She makes big, hopeful, spindy-bear eyes.

"No, I've been warning-triangle-orange my whole life," I say. "I'm sticking with the brown."

She grins. "Excellent. I need to do a color-touchup for my final exam, and you're perfect."

She's been trying to get me to volunteer all term, but I'm not sure putting my appearance into the hands of a complete novice is the best idea. Still, she's got a full term behind her now, and I've seen some of her other victims. I nod.

Kara squeals and grabs my hand, dragging me toward the Esthet-i-lab. It's just beyond Luberick, so I don't have time to change my mind.

"I'm ready," Kara announces to the man standing at a desk just inside the building. "I've got a client."

He nods, swiping something on his holo-screen. "Third door on the left," he says, giving me a bland look. Is that a pity?

My stomach flip-flops, making me wish I hadn't just eaten a celebratory meal at the Burger Hole.

"I THOUGHT you needed to do a touch-up. This isn't brown," I say, glaring at the tiny mirror Kara holds up. "This is red. And silver."

"But not your natural red." She gives me an innocent look. "This a Christmas red. You've got holiday party hair!"

"If I wanted to look like gift wrap, I would have mentioned that," I say, eyes narrowed. I glance at the mirror again, but the view hasn't changed. My hair hangs, ruler-straight, like a curtain against my cheek. Alternating stripes of red and silver glitter in the bright lights. Glitter!

"You know I'm not much of a holiday party girl," I say, my teeth clenched so tight I can feel my jaw seize up.

"Maybe it's time to change that." Kara sniffs, and busies herself putting away equipment. She takes off her pink TSTI lab coat and tosses it into the laundry shoot. "Come on, I need to have you graded, then I have the perfect idea!"

She drags me down the hall to her instructor's office. The instructor isn't here—she's probably on a beach on the Ebony Coast, drinking Jager Hula cocktails with my history of technology teacher. Seriously. Rumor has it, they've got a thing going.

Kara pushes me gently into the room, and I step onto a circular platform. A red light passes over my face, then rotates around my head. As we wait, numbers flick up onto a screen on the far wall, grading her on artistic vision, creativity, execution and a bunch of other scores that mean nothing to me.

Kara pumps an arm into the air and yells, "Yes! An A!" With a loud whoop, she grabs my arm and drags me out of the room.

When we pass the guy at the desk, he bites his lip, as if trying not to laugh. "Enjoy your break," he says, shaking his head, slowly. He mutters something that sounds like, "Poor girl."

"You, too!" Kara sings as she hurries me out the door. "Come on, let's get back to the dorm." She flicks her holo-ring and calls a robo-taxi. "My treat," she says when I start to complain about the cost. "It's Christmas! We have things to do."

THE NEXT MORNING, or maybe its afternoon, the next afternoon, I peel my sticky eyes open. Kara's voice warbles in a Christmas song over the shower. Her side of the room looks like a laundry shuttle decompressed over it.

I drag myself upright, holding my head. Too much Jager Hula is always my downfall. Vowing to never drink again, I stagger to my dresser and pull out a pain patch. Blessed relief pours through my head the moment I slap it onto my neck.

Kara comes out of the bathroom, her hair in a towel, a green robe with embroidered Christmas ornaments all over wrapped around her body. "I really wish you'd come home with me," she says. "Staying on campus over Christmas is as depressing as it gets."

I smile. "Thanks, but I don't think I could take a week at the Ortega Okilo compound. Too many people."

"Compound!" She laughs. "You mean hovel. And you'd have a great time! At least promise you'll come over for Christmas eve. I'll come get you." She gives me the spindy-bear eyes, again.

I sigh. "If you promise there won't be any Jager Hula shots, I'll come. And you don't have to come get me—I can get there on my own."

She squeezes me in a quick hug then narrows her eyes. "If you don't get there by 5pm, I'm sending my cousin Aloff to come get you. If you think I'm a party animal, wait until you meet Aloff. You'd be so drunk by the time you got to Christmas dinner, you wouldn't sober up until New Year's."

I hold up my hands. "No need to send Aloff. I'll be there, I promise."

THE TECHNOINST IS DESERTED over winter break. Literally. I'm the only person living on campus—technically the dorms are shut down, but I might have hacked the building locks. There's no food service, but I spent the last of my credits on cup noodles and dry cereal, so I haven't starved.

Christmas eve, I wake in a panic. I'm supposed to go to Kara's house for dinner tonight, and I don't have a gift. It's traditional, on Kaku, to bring something to your hosts when you show up for a meal.

I paw through my meager belongings, looking for something I can transform into a present. I've already created a holo-ring app for Kara—it pulls hair care product reviews off the net, then finds the cheapest place to buy knock-offs of the highest rated items. But I need something *physical* to give her mom.

No reason to panic. I have the whole day. Well, what's left of the day. I slept in a bit. Surely there must be something affordable and still available.

When I pull up my bank balance, though, my heart sinks. Two point seven eight credits. I knew I was broke, but yikes.

I dress in shorts and a t-shirt, grab my last protein bar, and lock the door behind me. I take the elevator out of the underground res-stack but get out one floor below the top. Instead of heading up to the front door, I detour to the maintenance room.

A flick of my holo-ring unlocks the door, and I skirt past the garaged cleaning gear to the access panel at the back. Since the campus is closed, building access doors are locked and monitored, so I have to take the back way in and out.

I open the cleaning hatch on the delivery chute and climb the ladder inside. When the building is in use, cleaning products are dumped down this chute into pods. Then the cleaning bots lock onto the pods to get their load of soap or solvent. I've used my hacking skills to check the delivery schedules, and this chute should be out of use until just after New Year's Day. With the building closed, there's no need for cleaning.

The rungs on the ladder are slippery with the last dump of detergent. But I've climbed in and out this way a few times over the last week, leaving clear spots for my hands and feet. Halfway to the top, a clang stops me in my tracks.

The metal walls of the chute shake, and the ladder creaks. The door just a couple meters above my head opens and light shines in.

My heart erupts into overtime, pounding blood through my ears. I can't be here when they deliver! I'll be flushed into the holding tank! I'll drown in a sudsy soup of citrus scented slop!

"Wrong chute!" a voice echoes against the metal above my head, and the door slams shut.

I close my eyes and breath deeply, clutching the ladder. That was too close. Maybe I should have gone home with Kara.

I STUMBLE out of the delivery chute and lean against the cold plascrete wall. The delivery drones are gone—I climbed back down and waited a good thirty minutes after the last rumbling clang rang through the walls.

I slide down the plascrete and sit on the dirty curb next to the delivery deck. A flick to my holo-ring brings up my bank account, again, but nothing has changed there. No Christmas miracle has deposited piles of treasure on my behalf. I probably have the skills to make some credits magically appear, but I'm not a thief.

After a few minutes, I get up and wander across the campus. Although the buildings are all closed, a few people sit on the grass or lounge on the benches in the afternoon sun. A red-haired girl waves at me. It's Lindsay— we met in a basic writing class. I wave back, but don't stop to chat.

Flashing my student ID at the payment panel in the T-bahn station, I ride the deserted slide ramp down to the platform. Hot, metallic air blows my tinsel-hair away from my face as the train pulls to a stop.

The car is deserted, and I sink onto one of the worn plastek seats. Just before the doors close, two guys and a girl squeeze in, speaking quickly in a language I don't understand. They look at me, then hurry to the far end of the car. Based on their jeans and scruffy t-shirts, they're probably students, too.

We all get off at transfer station and then board the same train to Réalta. When the train pulls out, one of the boys approaches me.

"Hello. My name is Cas." The tinny voice of a cheap translator comes through my audio implant. "You look like holiday star." He points at an advertisement flashing on the screen by the door. A red and silver striped star leads wise shoppers to a big sale at Joe's Furniture.

I clap my hand to my head. "Yeah, I know."

"We wondering if you help us."

I give him my best I'm-trying-to-be-nice-but-this-better-not-be-a-pickup-line smile. "What do you need help with?"

"We are lost," Cas says. "Melly said she had instructions, but she has not. Balt knows nothing." He looks down the train at his friends and they wave enthusiastically.

"Where are you trying to go?" I ask. Giving directions to lost visitors should get me some good karma. Maybe I'll find that gift I need.

"We visit our friend." Cas sits beside me, and his companions move closer. Slowly, as if they're worried they'll spook me. The way they creep up the car almost does. "The friend is for medical facility in Réalta."

"Do you have the name of the facility?" I ask. I haven't spent much time in Réalta, but I'm sure I can find directions. I flick my holo-ring and pull up a mapping app. "What's it called?"

"This is problem," Melly says, from the seat beside me.

I jump. A second ago, she was three rows back. Now she's right next to me.

"I have lost name." She pats her pockets. "Is on paper, but no is nowhere."

"Why didn't you put it into your holo-map?" I ask, gesturing to the transparent map hovering over my palm. But none of them are wearing holo-rings. Maybe they use old-style communication tablets?

"We have not this device," Balt says.

My head snaps around. He's sitting right in front of me. These folks are ninja-sneaky. "No holo-rings? No comtabs?"

They all hold up their empty hands. "Only paper," Balt says, waving a scrap.

"Is that the address?" I ask reached for it. He lets me take it, but it's only an advertisement for a holiday craft fair. I look on both sides, thinking he might have written it down, but nothing. When I try to hand it back, he waves me off.

I drop the paper on the seat next to me and pull up a search. "Let's see, there are—crap."

All six eyes lock onto me.

"Yes?" they say in unison.

"Fourteen medical centers in Réalta." The scents of cinnamon and resin tickle my nose. I rub it. "Do you have contact info? Or at least a name?"

They look at each other, then all three heads shake.

"Wait, you said this is a friend," I say. "You don't know his name?"

"Her," they say together.

"She is Miriam," Balt says. "But other names are unknown."

"Why do you have to visit this woman if you don't know her?" I ask.

"We were told to visit," Melly says. "By the elders. So, we must."

The other nod, like bobblehead toys.

"The elders?" I ask.

"Our elders," Cas says. "They said when we are on Kaku, we must visit. And bring gifts."

All three reach into their pockets and pull out...things. Things that shouldn't have fit into their jeans' pockets.

Melly holds a large gold, metallic box. It's square-cornered, with a lock on the front and ornate filigree on the lid. She holds it carefully in both hands, as if it is heavy.

I look, but don't touch.

Cas lifts an ancient-looking jar. The glass is thick and green, and small, uneven chunks of something rattle inside as he raises it. A worn cork plugs the top, tied on with a thin silver rope that loops around the neck of the jar and over the top. The bits inside look like candied gingeh-root.

Balt holds out a polished wooden box. It's bigger than Melly's and has iron handles on each end. The top and sides are carved in thick relief, but I can't tell what it depicts. I catch a glimpse of animals and an angel and a star. An astringent smell hits my nose—it reminds me of needle trees.

I nod. "Those look like appropriate Christmas gifts," I say.

They smile and the gifts disappear. Not like "poof" they're gone, but as if they've been hidden away somewhere on their bodies. But all three of them are wearing tight jeans and t-shirts. Nowhere to hide more than a few coins or a scrap of paper.

"Will you help us?" Melly asks.

"I'll try," I say, flicking through the clinic listings. "Do you know why she's in the clinic? Maybe we can eliminate some of these. Is she injured?"

The three confer quickly in their quiet, liquid language. For some reason, the translator doesn't work. Then all three heads shake.

"Not injured," I say. I guess I can eliminate the emergency room. Unless —"Is she sick? Food poisoning?"

More head shakes. "That's right, you said the elders told you to visit—when did they tell you? Recently?"

"Before we left home," Cas says. "Many days."

"Weeks," Balt says.

I look from one to the other. "Which is it? Days or weeks?"

"Weeks," says Cas.

"Days," Balt says at the same time.

I turn to Melly. She's sitting across the aisle now, although I didn't see her move. My eyes narrow. "What kind of game are you trying to pull? I don't have any money, so there's no point in trying to shake me down." I pat my pockets, but aside from my holo-ring, there's nothing they can take.

"No!' Melly says. "We are not shake you down. Miriam is bringing baby. The elders tell us many weeks—" she shoots a glare at the boys "—to visit. They say she have baby days after we here."

Ah! A baby. There are only three birthing centers listed, so that narrows the search a bit. I give her a considering look.

She smiles, hopefully, doing the spindy-bear eyes just like Kara. Kara! Maybe she can help. She lives in Réalta.

"My friend lives near here," I say, glancing up at the locator blinking above the door. "The next stop. Let's get off there, and maybe she can help us find the right place."

The three of them cheer, and the train slides into the Réalta station. Balt leaps off a seat at the front of the train—when did he move? And why was he crouching on the seat? They all dance off the train, jigging and chanting something in their beautiful foreign tongue.

We take the slideway to the surface and push through the revolving glass door. It's gotten dark already, and the main square of Réalta is unrecognizable—glittering in lights and decorations. Glass baubles, sparkling crystals, shining colored projections cover every building on all sides. The effect is dazzling—even in the day, it must be astounding.

In the center of the huge plaza, a tree stands. It towers above the space, with a bright star glowing on the top. Melly, Balt, and Cas stop and stare.

"This is regular?" Balt asks, pointing to the tree.

My brown furrow. "You mean is there always a tree here? No, I think it's for Christmas."

They nod, as if I've said something profound. "This way," says Balt. He strides across the square toward the tree.

"Where's he going?" I ask Melly.

"He knows," Cas says, following Balt. Melly nods emphatically and hurries after them.

"He knows what?" I ask, running to keep up. "Did he remember the address?"

They stride across the plaza, their steps increasing to a jog. Balt runs to the tree, then veers to the right, angling to one of the far corners. The others follow, singing again as they run. I stumble along in their wake, no longer certain why I'm bothering, but feeling compelled to stick with them to the end.

A narrow alley opens off the shadowed corner of the square. Balt points to a bright blue door, with a star-shaped lamp shining above it. Swirling symbols picked out in gold sparkle on a blue sign. I snap a pic with my holo-cam and run it through my translator.

"Birthing Center," it reads.

Melly grabs my hand and pulls me through the open door into a cool room. The boys run to a tall desk and chatter at the man standing behind it. He says something and points to an interior door.

"She's here," Cas says. "You found her."

They're all looking at me. "I didn't do anything," I say. "I just got off the train. But I'm glad you found your friend. I should go."

"No, you must come with us!" Balt and Melly take my hands, and Cas closes in behind, urging me through the interior door. It should feel creepy and forced, but instead it's as though I've been offered something precious.

We walk down a quiet hall lit by faux candles in sconces between closed doors. At the far end, a door stands ajar. Inside, a shabby bed with a worn quilt takes up most of the room. A young woman sits on the bed, a tiny baby bundled in her arms. The young man sitting on the edge of the bed stands as we enter, stepping back to give us room.

Melly moves to the bed and leans forward, kissing the woman—Miriam —on each cheek. Then she kisses the baby's head. She says something, soft and melodic, and places her golden box on the bed. Each of the boys does the same, mimicking her movements exactly.

When all three gifts have been presented, they draw me forward. "This is our final gift," Melly says, and the translator works now, for some reason. "A gift to us. She led us to you."

The woman's eyes meet mine, and a rush of love pours through me. I gasp, my breath sucked out of my lungs. Tears prick my eyes and one trickles down my cheek. I don't know what just happened. I suck in a deep breath.

She holds out the baby. The truth is I'm not much of a baby person, so I smile and make appropriate noises, nodding at Miriam. She locks eyes with me, then looks down at the baby and holds him out again.

Puzzled, I look down. The baby is swaddled in a blue blanket. She pushes him toward me. I take the baby, holding him in my elbow. He's so tiny, I could almost hold him in one hand. A feeling of calm comes over me, my body relaxing muscles I hadn't realized were tense. The baby opens his eyes and looks up at me, solemn and trusting. I smile and kiss his forehead.

Finally, I hand the baby back to his mother. "I'm glad your friends were able to find you."

"We always find that for which we are searching," she says through the tinny translator. "Blessings to you."

Melly, Balt and Cas usher me out of the room. The door closes softly behind us. "Where are you staying?" I ask.

Balt shakes his head. "We don't stay. The train takes us to the spaceport."

"You came all this way, and now you're leaving again? Do you want to come to my friend's house for dinner? She said they always have way too much food, and they're expecting me—oh, crap! I'm late!"

We hurry out of the building. I start across the square, then look back. There's no one in sight.

For a moment I stare around the plaza, but I see only well-dressed people hurrying to Christmas parties. No trio of scruffy teens in tight jeans and t-shirts. The blue door is hidden in the shadows, the light off. I squint, but I can't make out the sign or the star-shaped fixture above it.

Overhead, a clock bell rings. I am really late! I hurry down the street and around the corner. The tall houses here are tight against each other, making the streets into narrow canyons. Surprisingly, Kara's home is just around the corner from the square. I don't remember coming this way last time I visited.

When I reach Kara's house, the doors are open and music flows out like water. A tall blond guy stands on the doorstep, his back to me.

"Fine, I'm getting her," he says. "But don't wait up! I have a party tonight." He turns.

"You must be Aloff," I say, holding out my hand. "Triana Moore."

He grins, showing off crooked teeth in an endearing smile. "I'm supposed to get you, but I guess I'm off the hook. Don't tell Aunt Larin you saw me!" He gives me a fist bump and disappears between the buildings. A cool breeze pushes in behind me, following Aloff through the street.

"Triana!" Kara cries, coming to the door. "You made it! I just sent Aloff for you."

"He must have gone the other way," I say, pointing the way he'd gone.

"That *is* the most direct way to the train station," she says.

"It is?" I look behind me. "But the station is just around that corner."

She gives me a funny look. "No."

"In the big square." I jog back to the corner and peer around it. No square. More houses, with Christmas revelers, but no train station, or massive tree, or blue door. I stare at Kara, flummoxed.

"Triana!" Kara's mom, Larin, comes to the door. She steps onto the doorstep and rubs her arms, looking up at the sky. "It's gotten cool, hasn't it?" She looks at me. "Thank you for the beautiful flowers."

"What flowers?" I follow her into the house.

She points to an amazing arrangement on a side table. They look like they were specially designed to coordinate with the rest of the home's Christmas decorations.

I pull the card from the basket.

To the Ortega Okilo Family.

Thank you for your hospitality.

Triana Moore.

On the back is the business name: Weizman Florists. There's no address or contact information. Underneath, in tiny letters, someone has written in C + M + B.

"Where is Weizman Florists?" Larin asks. "I haven't heard of them before."

Neither have I. Their shop is probably on the square that doesn't seem to exist anymore. Maybe right next to the blue door.

By the window, Kara screeches. "Snow!"

"WHAT?!" Everyone in the house bolts for the windows.

"Snow!"

"The weather feed didn't say anything about snow!"

"Aloff must be up on the roof."

We tumble out into the street. A brisk wind blows through the canyon formed by the tall houses. Huge white flakes drift down, settling on hair and clothing, melting on warm skin.

"How can it be snowing?" Kara wonders. "It never snows in Realta!"

I shrug. "Freak snowstorm?" Caused by the three Weizman?

Before I can say anything, Kara throws her arms around me. "Merry Christmas, Triana!"

"Merry Christmas, Kara."

IN MANY COUNTRIES, on Epiphany—the first Sunday of the new year—the "three kings" visit homes and mark the front door with chalk. The blessing usually includes the year, as well, so this year it would be "20 + C + M + B +22."

Traditionally, C + M + B refer to the names of the three Wise Men who visited the Holy Family at the Nativity: Caspar, Melchior and Balthasar — who gifted the infant Jesus with gold, frankincense and myrrh.

It also is an abbreviation for the Latin *Christus mansionem benedicat*, which translates to "Christ bless this home."

When we lived in Germany, teenaged boys would dress as the three kings. They walked around the village, cranking a wooden device that made clacking noises to alert the town to their arrival. For a small donation, they would bless your house. The money was given to the poor.

Now, the Bible doesn't list the names of the wise men—or even mention how many there were. But I'm not going to argue with 2000 years of tradition.

I hope you enjoyed this Christmas story. I wish you a healthy, happy and prosperous year.

AUTHOR'S NOTE

Thanks for reading these short stories. The first two are part of the "complete" Triana Moore Space Janitor series. But they aren't available in print, so I bundled them, along with the bonus story, to create a printable book.

If you're looking for other books I've written—and if you're still reading, I guess you enjoy my style—check out my web page. I've continued Triana's stories in the Tales of a Former Space Janitor series, and I've got several other series as well. You can sign up for my newsletter on my website juli ahuni.com. I send it out every other Sunday. You'll get news about what I've been doing, a couple of free short stories, and information about other books that you might like.

Thanks for taking the time to read all this. Thanks to my family and my editor (my cousin, so also family!) for supporting me on this journey. And thanks to the Big Guy who makes all things possible.

ALSO BY JULIA HUNI

Printed in Great Britain
by Amazon